COASTAL SPIRIT

LINDSAY MARIE MILLER

Chapter 1

What was that?" Louisa turned back and looked off into the distance, gazing through the trees.

Frederic walked in a straight line and lifted his head to the sky. Billows of smoke danced and swirled across a tapestry that belonged to the clouds. A strange breeze drifted through the trees, lightly jostling every green leaf.

When Frederic looked back at Louisa, she draped her arms over her stomach in a comforting hug. He knew that he had chosen the wrong time to say those things to her. That they could never be together. That she was all wrong for him. That he loved her anyway.

But Frederic only wanted to protect her from a life of worry. Days spent trapped beneath a ceiling of poverty. If they ever made it back to New York, Frederic refused to entertain the thought of a life with Ms. Louisa Rochester. He had nothing to offer her, and she deserved the whole world. He could not marry Louisa, because she would just end up hating him in the end if he did.

With her blue eyes burning bright, Louisa gazed up at Frederic and waited. She waited for him to say he was sorry, that he never meant any of those things. She waited for him to draw near and hold her close. But he did not, and Louisa failed to understand why she was filled with just as much surprise as disappointment.

"Why don't we look for that cat of yours and find out?" Frederic grinned at Louisa, but she did not return the expression.

Instead, she brushed past him with her head down, resenting the fact that her body trembled when it came so close to his. She cupped her elbows in her palms and heard his footsteps at her back. A single tear streamed down her cheek, her last one, as Louisa sought out whatever had been the source of that explosive sound.

After five minutes of silence, Frederic could not bear the absence of her smile. "Louisa," he called after her. But she neither stopped nor turned to face him.

Frederic stared at the back of her pretty blonde head, knowing that he would never be able to get her out of his. She was just a girl, a child, just sixteen. But he couldn't help viewing her as the beautiful grown woman that she was destined to become.

"Louisa!" Frederic rose his voice, and she hurried her steps in retaliation. She refused to let

Praise for *EMERALD GREEN*

"I loved this book! ...one of the best romance novels I have read in a while"

—Nerd Girl

"...this one definitely hit the spot. I can't wait for the next book...!"

—Kylie's Fiction Addiction

"This book was all kinds of amazing. I loved every word of it. Sooo good!"

—Amazon Reviewer

"I can't wait to get my hands on the next book. I need more!!"

—Amazon Reviewer

"This book is awesome! I can't wait to read what happens in the next story."

—Amazon Reviewer

"This author is incredibly talented... This was an amazing five star read! This book was SO good! I can't wait to see what happens next in the series!!"

—Amazon Reviewer

DON'T MISS THESE OTHER BOOKS BY
LINDSAY MARIE MILLER

The Girl in the Woods

Emerald Green

Honey Gold

Me & Mr. Jones

Mr. Jones & Me

Jungle Eyes

Island Smile

Single

An Arrangement

An Accident

Mercy

AND LOOK FOR HER NEW NOVEL
Available in January 2018

him see the way his words had affected her. She would rather die than give him the pleasure of watching her in pain.

Soon, her quick march transcended to stomping, and she wasn't even embarrassed by it. Perhaps he should have thought twice before plunging a dagger straight through her fragile heart. Metaphorically speaking, of course.

"Louisa!" Frederic repeated for the third time. "Will you just wait?"

She ignored him and marched faster, wanting to be away from the man who had claimed her broken heart. Somehow, this was worse than discovering that Captain William Pierce was actually a pirate named Judas. His affection for her had been a fraud, but Frederic's was real.

Frederic grabbed her arm and pulled her back, holding her wrists when she squirmed. "What would you prefer? That I lie to you?"

"Yes," Louisa snapped. She attempted to scurry away from him, but he would not let her go.

"So you'd love a liar then?" he challenged her, smoothing his thumb along the inside of her wrist.

"I would rather believe that you hate me with every fiber of your being than know that you love me and we cannot be together."

Frederic released her and blinked the sunlight from his eyes. "Fine." Then he took a step closer at the very moment she took a step back. "I hate you," he said. "I hate your long blonde hair and your blue eyes." His hands came around her face as he tilted her head back. "I hate the way you look at me. I hate the way you smile."

As her lower lip trembled, Frederic brushed his finger against the plump, soft nature of it. She stood there helpless and vulnerable before him. Her heart was beating so fast that it melted her insides to the consistency of sweet honey and molasses.

"I hate the way you say my name," Frederic went on. Her eyes were locked on his, and he knew that was where he wanted them to be. Always.

Louisa shivered, because the blood beneath her skin was pulsing with delight. "Go on," she softly requested. "Please."

Frederic threaded his fingers through her hair and brought his face closer to hers. "I hate the way you say I love you."

Louisa was glued to the spot by the earnest look in his sparkling gray eyes. They almost looked metallic today. Like silver.

"What else?" she whispered.

"I hate the way it feels to hold you in my arms at night."

"How does it feel?" she wondered, her voice turning soft and sweet.

"Like heaven," he crooned, gently caressing her skin.

Louisa whimpered at the very moment Frederic molded his mouth to hers. Her fingers traveled across the fabric of his shirt, and his chest tightened at her touch. Frederic was delicate and tender as he angled her face to meet every kiss.

Longing for the body of the girl he could never have, Frederic let his hands drift to her waist. When he pulled back an inch to let her breathe, Louisa cooed. Her eyes remained closed but she smiled, clinging to the collar of his shirt.

Frederic rubbed his hand over Louisa's hair and grinned when a fresh shade of blush stained her cheeks. Sinking her teeth into her lower lip, Louisa opened her eyes and stared into Frederic's. She could not help herself when her gaze immediately landed on his mouth. Her heart thrummed against her chest, and Louisa knew that she wanted him to kiss her like that again.

But something caught Louisa's eye, as she reluctantly pulled her focus from Frederic for a moment. In the distance, molten hot lava was searing across the land, melting everything in its path like candle wax. "Frederic," she gasped, tugging at his sleeve.

Frederic followed Louisa's line of sight, and his eyes shot wide open with alarm. A gushing lake of lava came rushing towards them. "Run!"

Paralyzed by the sight, Louisa faltered in her steps, fumbling about from the very start. Frederic grabbed Louisa by the arm and dragged her after him. But she looked back, mesmerized by the thick viscous nature of running lava.

"Louisa, let's go!" Frederic barked. "Come on!" He sprinted through the trees, twisting her arm when she failed to run fast enough.

"Move!" he shouted when the lava nearly touched their heels.

At the first sign of the ocean, Frederic darted to the left and yanked Louisa after him. He cut through the jungle and slipped out of the lava's path just in time. When they reached the sand on the beach, Frederic checked over his shoulder to make sure they had dodged the line of fire.

Louisa let go of his hand and stumbled to the ground on her hands and knees at the shoreline. She coughed and grasped her stomach, worried that she might gag. A sleek sheen of ice cold sweat coated her skin at the thought of drowning in scorching hot lava.

Frederic waded out into the ocean and sat down beside her, letting the salty waves rush over them. They exchanged a look that communicated every word they had yet to say. Louisa sailed into his arms and held on tight, still struggling to catch her breath.

Pulling her in closer, Frederic stroked his fingers through Louisa's hair and cradled her head to his chest. When she calmed down, Frederic kept her tangled in his embrace. Then he looked back and spotted the purging volcano off in the distance.

Still shuddering in fear, Louisa crawled into his lap and dug her nails in at the back of his neck. Frederic relaxed as she placed her head on his shoulder and breathed in and out. Like a coping mechanism for the potential death they had just skirted around. In truth, the volcano had been one of many close calls that never seemed to be very far away.

How many lives did they have left? How many more times could they cheat death? How many days remained on the island for them to survive?

Chapter 2

Fleeing like the coward he was, Judas hopped to his feet and took off into the jungle. Rather than racing towards the beach, he rushed inland. Perhaps he believed that the deeper he plunged into the forest, the greater his chance of survival.

Relieved, yet confused by the sudden departure of Judas, Elaine sat up on her knees. Her hands were shaking and unyielding fear trembled through her body. When she turned to look back, Elaine's mouth hung gaping open and her eyes widened in shock. Lava skied down the volcano with precision and speed, quickly making its way towards them.

Sure to be quick, Elaine glanced down and spotted the knife and pistol on the ground. Judas had been enough of a scared fool to run off and leave without them. She scooped the weapons up in her hands and hurried over to Henry with them.

"Henry," she called, shaking his shoulders. But

he would not wake up. "Henry!"

Elaine peered over her shoulder, but the lava had yet to filter through the trees. Regardless, it was inevitably on its way and heading towards them. Fast.

"Wake up, Henry!" Elaine cried, trying her best to stay strong and not fall apart. When he made no movement, Elaine darted her eyes over his peaceful face.

Henry was unconscious and bleeding with a gunshot wound in the leg. If Elaine couldn't move him, the lava would swallow him whole and he would be buried alive.

"HENRY, PLEASE!" She begged, jerking his arms and shoulders. "Wake up, my love. Please, wake up."

When Henry lay still, Elaine flicked her eyes up at the rushing lava in the distance. Then she turned back to Henry and slapped him across the face. But even that would not rouse him from his state of sleep.

"Dammit, Henry," Elaine muttered, her teeth clacking together with fear. She reached over and grabbed the dagger, then sat back on her knees and looked at him. "I am sorry, my love." Elaine molded her mouth to his and then fought through the tears in her eyes. "I'm sorry."

With a shaky hand, Elaine opened Henry's palm and sliced the blade along his skin. At the sudden pain, Henry shot up and yelled. He glanced down at his bloody hand and turned to

Elaine in shock.

"Get up!" Elaine commanded when his right foot made contact with the ground. The bloody gunshot wound in his calf was pulsing and red. "Come on, Henry. Move!"

Gritting his teeth, Henry clung to Elaine's arm and hopped forward on his left foot. He limped on the right, not daring to bring the full weight of his body down on it.

"Henry!" Elaine squealed, as a sea of fiery orange lava came rushing towards them.

Elaine dug her fingernails into the back of Henry's shirt and tore her eyes away from the volcano, pushing onward through the jungle. Despite his agony, Henry felt the bordering heat and took off on his bare feet. With every step, Henry clenched his teeth so tight that he thought they might crack. But he would rather watch the bone in his leg pierce through his skin than drown in a hot lake of fire and lava.

Ducking and weaving through the forest, Elaine clamped her hand onto Henry's arm and refused to let go. When they created enough distance, Elaine turned back and looked over her shoulder at the all-consuming, molten hot liquid fire. Henry sat down in the grass, yet to be touched and charred by the volcano. It was somewhat fascinating to watch a sea of blood and fire, for that was how it looked. It sent a chill up Elaine's spine, and even though the lava was flaming hot, she felt terrifyingly cold.

"We must go, Henry." Elaine knelt down and clasped Henry's elbow, thankful that they had missed the lava lake. If Henry had remained unconscious, Elaine had no clue how she would have been able to save him. Henry had a gunshot wound that needed to be treated. Lacking confidence, Elaine worried that she might not possess the skills to mend his wound. Unlike the time Jade had flayed Henry's torso with claw marks, a bullet was currently in his body, saturated in his blood.

So many things could go wrong. What if the injury became inflamed? What if the injury became infected? As her mind raced with fear, Elaine wrapped Henry's arm around her shoulder and let him lean into her body for support. She curled her arm around his waist and led him through the forest, while Henry hopped on one foot, sweating with discomfort and fear.

A cool breeze drifted through the trees as Elaine looked out for the approaching sea. Henry gasped and grunted, struggling to carry himself along. How she longed to have the strength of a grown man, someone who could lift Henry up and carry him to shore. But Henry was simply too heavy for her to do anything more than drag him. Since he insisted on hobbling his way there, Elaine filed the possibility away as a last resort.

"Elaine." Henry winced, a fine line of sweat streaking down his face. "I must stop to rest."

Concerned for her husband, Elaine slowed to a

stop and eased Henry into a seated position on a flat stone. When his posterior connected with the rock, Henry dug his heels into the ground and leaned back with a hiss. Then he flicked the stray pieces of dark hair from his face and lowered his head to examine the gunshot wound in his leg.

Not wanting to rush Henry, Elaine crouched down before him and rubbed his arm to provide some sense of comfort. When he looked up at her, fear flitted across Henry's light golden eyes. Perhaps he had already begun to consider what his future life may hold.

"Henry," Elaine called, taking his face in her hands. "Let me take you to shore. I can mend it. Just like the time you were attacked by Jade when you first arrived on the island."

Licking his lower lip, Henry looked off into the distance and then settled his gaze on Elaine. "Yes, but your jungle cat did not have claws made of bullets."

Elaine hung her head and squeezed his arm. She had already thought as much, but was too afraid to say anything to him. Should he drown in the helplessness of doom?

"I know, Henry." Elaine got down on her knees and peered up into his eyes. "But I can fix it," she assured him. It was stretching the truth, but how could she frighten him? How could she entertain the thought of the damaging effects of that single bullet?

"Thank you, my love. But what about

infection?" Henry smoldered.

"Henry, I can prevent it from being infected. It is still early on."

Henry shook his head and growled. "Oh, really? And how, Elaine? You are not a doctor. You have no medical experience," he snapped, raising his voice.

"I know, Henry," she spoke in a still, small voice. "But I can—"

"What? What can you do?" he shouted, alarming Elaine. "Forget infection, darling. What if it becomes gangrenous? Have you ever thought of that?"

"No, I hadn't thought of it." She bowed her head in supplication, praying for a sense of healing calm to drift through his body. In all honesty, she had thought of it. But she was just so happy to have escaped the volcano and still have him alive. For now, at least.

"We are trapped here on this godforsaken island, and I could very well spend my final days here as a man with one leg!" Henry yelled, his face flushed with red ripe anger.

Her skin prickled at the sound of his words. In all their time as man and wife, Henry had never frightened Elaine to such a degree. She had known of his temper from the moment he arrived on the island, but never expected to hear such rage as this.

Henry refused to see light in the matter, letting nothing but darkness filter his thoughts. As warm tears streamed down from Elaine's eyes, she swiftly wiped them away with her fingertips. There was a hole in her chest where her heart used to be.

"Elaine." Henry reached out to touch her shoulder, but she moved away.

Letting her raven black locks fall in her face, Elaine rose to her feet and walked several steps away with her back to him. She shut her eyes and took a deep breath, picturing the life she had envisioned them to have. It was surely a fantasy now, no more than a dream. Henry and Elaine in New York with little Lilly in a stroller on a warm spring walk in Central Park. The mental image shattered, and Elaine broke down into sobs.

Sinking to the ground, Elaine touched the base of the nearest tree and wept. She got down on her knees and leaned into the trunk, finding more warmth in the wood than her husband could provide. A thick lump nestled at the bottom of her throat, tangling and twisting her stomach into knots. All Elaine really wanted to do was scream.

Henry braided his fingers together and stared at the ground. When he looked over at Elaine crying, turmoil ripped through his heart, because he had hurt the one he held most dear. He pressed his fingertips against his temple and let out a sorrowful sigh.

"Elaine," he called, but there was no reply. "Elaine, I'm sorry."

Elaine tilted her head to the side, though only enough for her to hear him. Then she tucked a lock of hair behind her ear and flitted her eyes across the forest floor.

"Darling," Henry whispered, seeing the fault in his outrage. "Please."

Elaine bit her lower lip and trembled, butting her forehead against the palm of her hand. After making love to Henry and then nearly being raped by Judas, and fleeing a sea of lava from the volcano only to realize that her husband may never walk again, Elaine's sheer sanity was moments away from shattering. She was a mere human, who could only bear so much.

Henry stood up and hopped over to the tree by Elaine. Despite the pain in his leg, he leaned into the trunk and took a seat behind her, plagued with guilt over what he had said.

"Elaine," he called, resting his hand on her back.

She flinched at his touch, which made him resent his actions all the more.

"Forgive me, darling," he gently crooned, brushing her hair over her shoulders. "I didn't mean what I said. Any of it. Can you just forget that I said it? I was upset."

Feeling mellow, Elaine sniffled at her sobs and took a deep breath.

Henry wrapped his arm around Elaine's stomach and placed his head on her shoulder. "I never want to hurt you," he reminded her. "Please believe me, my love."

Still shaking with the fear of losing him, Elaine

turned back and fell into his arms. Henry rubbed her back and held her close, making a mental note to never let his booming rage explode like that before her again. After all, how often did he have to run from lava?

Elaine stroked her fingers along the nape of Henry's neck and leaned back to look at him. "I thought surely he would kill you, and if you knew what he was about to do to me..."

Henry touched her hair and held her head up with his hands. "What did he do to you?" With a pounding heart in his chest, Henry pressed his thumb against her chin and then stroked the length of her jawline. "Elaine. Did he touch you?"

Elaine covered her mouth with her hand and cried, "Yes."

His golden eyes widened in a vengeful rage. But before he could take off on a mission to kill, Elaine grabbed the collar of his shirt until he was forced to stay.

"Not in the way you must think, Henry," she confessed. "But he wanted to. He was about to. If not for the volcano, it could have been so much worse."

Henry wiped all of her tears away and reeled Elaine into his lap.

"No, Henry. Your leg," she protested, concerned for his injury.

"Shh..." Henry brushed his finger across her lips. "I will be fine."

She looked into his eyes as he put her down on

his thigh, well away from the gunshot wound in his lower calf. Elaine gasped for air and embraced Henry, squeezing him with all of her might. Soaking up her love, Henry threaded his fingers through her hair and smelled her sweet, exotic scent. Then she brushed her cheek against his beard and sat up to look at him.

"Forget what I said before," Henry murmured. "I know you can mend my wounds."

With a tender smile, Elaine leaned in and covered his mouth with hers. Henry braided his hands at the small of her back and tugged at her lower lip, holding her body closer. When Elaine twisted her fingers through the ends of his hair and whimpered, Henry took a breath and rested his forehead against hers.

For the longest moment, they reveled in the warmth of holding each other close. Elaine could have been raped and killed. Henry could have been roasted alive. Either could have reached the end of life without the luxury of saying goodbye to the other.

When Elaine breathed him in and sighed, Henry tucked her head beneath his chin and lovingly caressed her arm. He ignored the throbbing, searing ache in his leg and channeled all of his pain towards the task of holding her close. As she snuggled into his warm body, Henry kissed her head and swept his fingers through her hair.

He was her savior. And she was his.

Chapter 3

Frederic circled his palm over Louisa's back as salty waves washed over them. She lowered her head as he traced lines across her face, his fingertips caressing every inch of skin with delicate care. Shock evaded them. Stone cold shock. And fear.

"We're never going to make it off this island," Louisa muttered. Her eyes stayed down as she contemplated the probable future laid out before her. Even if she never returned to New York City, she could still have a husband, a family, a life. Couldn't she?

"Sweet Louisa." Frederic turned her chin in his direction and willed her to look his way. As soon as he saw those innocent blue eyes, Frederic parted his lips to speak. "I wish you wouldn't say such things. You have a young, beautiful life ahead of you." Then he threaded his fingers through her hair and leaned closer. "For that is what you are."

Melancholy, Louisa turned her head to the

side and looked away from him. Tears threatened to break free and skitter down her cheeks, betraying her feelings on the inside. But Louisa fought against them and replied, "So I am worthy of a beautiful life, just not one with you." She darted her eyes up to meet his, holding her jaw taut with aggravation.

Frederic looked down at the waves around them and sighed. "You could never have the life you deserve, if you chose one with me." He took her hands and squeezed them. "Why can't you see, Louisa?" When he searched her eyes, she refused to meet his. "Don't you understand?"

"Understand what?" Louisa snapped, jerking her hands from his grasp. "That if matters were different... If I were older, If I were beautiful, If I were someone else, then what?" She narrowed her eyes at him, swallowing to ease the sudden dryness in her throat. "Then you would want me? Then I would be acceptable according to your rules?"

Frederic took her face in his hands, holding it merely inches from his own. Her eyes drifted from his full lips to his steely gray eyes, as she opened her mouth to speak.

"I don't deserve you," he whispered, struggling to get the words out.

Louisa gazed into his eyes without holding back. "I don't care."

Frederic touched her cheek and cocked his head to the side. When his fingertips descended to her neck, she lowered her lashes and sighed. But despite the pulsing desire racing across the surface of his body, Frederic felt obliged to be a gentleman.

"What do you want from me, girl?" he wondered. "You know I can never have you."

Opening her eyes, Louisa angled her cheek into the curve of his palm. "And what if we never leave this island? What if we are stranded here forever? No longer bound by the conventions of modern society. Like Adam and Eve. What do you make of us then?"

When the little angel put it like that, what was Frederic waiting for? He glanced at the deep blue sea and figured the chances of them returning home to New York alive. What if neither of them ever made it back? What if they were stuck in paradise forever? Together?

Would it be so wrong to indulge in his desire? What was so awful with the way he felt about Louisa Rochester? She was young. She was beautiful. She was innocent.

Louisa was perfectly pure in every sense of the word. From her flawless ivory complexion to those dazzling blue eyes that brightened every time he crossed her path. She was like a precious gemstone, untainted by the rough hands of another. Frederic hoped and dreamed and glimpsed his future in her eyes. But was that what she truly wanted?

Stranded on the island, Frederic could fulfill his dream and claim the one he truly loved: her.

New York City might remain a distant memory for all he knew. But the jungle posed no standards of high society. In the wild, there was no rich or poor, no young or old, no damaged or pure.

Nature, as colorful as it may seem, was black and white to say the least.

He was a man. She was a woman. There was no other point in the matter.

If Frederic and Louisa were trapped in paradise, why not find some pleasure in the pain? Why not enjoy the ever-blossoming nature of forbidden love?

Louisa touched the end of her nose to his cheek and then whispered in his ear. "I want you to touch me. I want you to love me. I want you to hold me close and never let go."

Solidified by her words, Frederic shut his eyes and treasured the feel of her lips above his neck. When he wrapped his arms around her and squeezed, Louisa trailed her fingertips along the ends of his hair and tugged. For so long, he had resisted the girl of his dreams, the angel in the night, the beautiful blonde beauty. But maybe he had been a fool.

After all, what was Frederic fighting? Desire? Lust? Attraction? The way she made him feel, because a civilization which he may never see the likes of again had led him to believe so?

Perhaps it was time to break the chain he had secured around his heart. Distance had never been intended for someone like Louisa, for she had breached the very walls and climbed straight over with the intent to mark him as her own. Body and Soul.

She had transfixed him from the very start. The young girl with the innocent blue eyes. Call it fate, destiny, or chance. But her charms were no accident.

They were in love.

"Frederic," Louisa whined, planting a soft kiss on his cheekbone.

Giving in, Frederic lifted her body up in his arms and Louisa wrapped her legs around him. Waves rolled onto the shore, crashing against them as Frederic worshipped her with a soul-stirring kiss. Louisa whimpered at the taste of his mouth and jerked at the collar of his shirt, bringing him as close to her as their bodies would allow.

Gentle and understanding, Frederic traced his hands over Louisa's back and returned his lips to hers. Despite the inevitability of what was bound to happen between them, Frederic wanted to take things slow. She would control the temperature and pacing of the undeniable passion between them. And Frederic would never take advantage of the situation or sweet Louisa. Because his wish had come true: all he ever wanted was her.

"Frederic," Louisa rasped against his mouth. "I love you."

He stilled at the sound of her words and frantic nature of her breathing. In a perfect world, Louisa would be his to keep forever and his father would be free. But when he took in the paradise surrounding them, maybe it wasn't as imperfect as it had seemed.

"And I love you," Frederic echoed.

Determined to go through matters right, Frederic put his hands on Louisa's face, and she clung to him to keep from falling out of his arms. He was so tall and strong and broad-shouldered, his body molded to muscular perfection. Desperate to receive his love, Louisa crushed her lips to his and leaned her head back when he began gifting kisses along the side of her face and down her neck. Nearly two decades alive, and all the glorious wonder of the world that she had missed. Surely, Frederic would enlighten her body and soul.

"Louisa?" a strangled, breathy voice called from afar.

Furrowing her brow at the familiar sound, Louisa lifted her head and looked up. Elaine stood in the sand with tears in her eyes, letting them stream down her face without caution. Alarm rippled through Louisa at the sight of her sister-in-law, the very woman she believed to be dead. If Elaine were still alive, then did that mean Henry...

Before she could finish her thought, Henry appeared in true living color and came hobbling towards her. Overwhelmed with joy, Louisa relaxed into Frederic's arms and beamed in delight.

Elaine was alive.

Henry was alive.

And they had found each other at last.

It was a miracle. Because now she could introduce them to her one true love, the dashing Frederic Holmes.

"How dare you!" Henry lunged forward and tackled Frederic into the ocean.

"Henry, no!" Louisa protested, but it was already too late. Her brother pounced on Frederic like wolves after a yearling. She held a hand to her gaping mouth and shook with grief as Henry pummeled Frederic and then held him down beneath the water.

"Elaine," Louisa cried, tugging on the dress of her sister-in-law. "Please. Make Henry stop. Don't let him hurt Frederic." She paused with a choking sob. "I love him."

Confused by the whole affair, Elaine looked from Louisa to Henry. Could it be that Frederic had not tortured and violated poor Louisa? Could he have beaten the odds and actually been kind? Could he have protected her instead? Maybe even loved her?

"Henry!" Elaine shouted, running into the ocean. "Henry, STOP!"

But Henry wrapped his hands around Frederic's neck and pushed his body beneath the water. The filthy scoundrel had put his hands all over Louisa. And he was going to pay.

"STOP!" Elaine waded into waist-deep water

and struggled to pull Henry back. "Stop it, Henry! You're going to kill him!" she warned, wrestling with what was true and right.

"Precisely." Henry lifted Frederic's head from the water and then dunked it below the surface again. Only this time, he had no intention of releasing his hold.

"Frederic!" Louisa shrieked. True terror flashed before her eyes as she watched her brother attempting to strangle the life out of the man she loved. As if sheer drowning weren't enough.

Unwilling to relinquish Frederic, Louisa rushed into the water and punched Henry in the face until he let go. As Frederic's body sank to the wet sand beneath the surface, Henry stumbled back and cried out in pain. Blood coated his teeth, and he could hardly believe that his own sister had broken his nose.

Elaine grabbed Henry by the arm and dragged him to shore, guiding his limping figure to the shelter of a shade tree where she could tend to his wounds properly.

Paralyzed with fear, Louisa grabbed the sleeve of Frederic's shirt and jerked him out of the water. When he fell limp in her arms, she dragged him to shore and lay his body down in the sand. Frantic and trembling, Louisa pressed her ear to his heart and then sat up to look at him. In a series of quick movements, she held his nose and performed mouth-to-mouth in a feeble attempt to revive him. As Frederic lay helpless in the wet sand beneath her, Louisa trembled and wept.

"Please, my darling. If you love me, come back to me," Louisa murmured.

When it seemed that her time had run out, Frederic finally lurched forward and coughed up water from the sea. Louisa dug her knees into the sand and beat him on the back, careful to hold him upright in a seated position.

When he could breathe again, Frederic briefly glanced over Louisa and then collapsed to the ground. He lay on the flat of his back and looked up into her eyes through the thin slits of his own. Sobbing with relief, Louisa placed her head on his chest and curled her body into his. Frederic responded to her touch by smoothing his hand across her shoulders, as she lay down beside him and listened to the sound of his beating heart.

Chapter 4

Have you gone mad?" Elaine snapped. After removing the bullet from Henry's leg and wrapping the wound in cloth, Elaine failed to overlook his erratic behavior.

"You know as well as I do that we have had every intention of killing that man."

"Yes, but did you ever see him harm her?" Elaine searched Henry's smoldering brown eyes when he looked away. His gaze inevitably landed on Frederic and Louisa curled up in the sand together. It was a strange picture to see the sister he loved so irrevocably tied to a man he had grown to hate. Regardless of the confusion, he had only intended to protect her.

Henry scowled and ground his teeth together in frustration.

"Did it ever occur to you that he might actually love her?" Elaine suggested.

"For goodness sake, Elaine." Henry gestured his hand across the way. "Frederic could be her father. He must be fifteen years her senior at least. What do you call that?"

"Henry," Elaine scolded. "She has been completely alone on this island, because we have been incapable of finding her. That man has saved her life on more than one occasion. And yes, if you must know, she loves him. She told me so herself."

Henry brushed the matter off with a sly shrug. "Louisa is sixteen," he explained. "Just the other day, she was professing her love for Judas. Look how much of a gentleman he turned out to be. Not that she would know any better."

"But what if Frederic is different?" Elaine turned soft and sweet, lowering her voice enough to sound sultry. When Henry met her glistening green eyes, he relaxed.

"Look, Elaine. I have no intention of apologizing to that man," he confessed. "Say what you want. But he is the one who brought her here to the island and took her away from home. How can I have any empathy for her captor?"

Elaine sank into the sand and replied, "Well, I think you should speak to them both."

"Do you now?" he answered back. "And why is that?"

"Because we all want the same thing."

"And what is that exactly?" Henry held his jaw taut and groveled.

"All four of us want Judas dead."

Surprised at the connection, Henry absorbed

her words and let his arms dangle over his knees. Perhaps she was right, but how could Frederic be trusted if that were the case? Did that not make him any more than a traitor?

"Just think reasonably about this, Henry. We've been apart on the island, and Judas has gained the upper hand every single time. Imagine if we formed an alliance. Perhaps Judas can take on two at a time. But how will he face up to four against one?"

Henry sighed in disapproval and shook his head from side to side. When he turned his head to gaze out along the shoreline, he found Louisa helping Frederic to his feet. The man was tall, strong, broad-shouldered, a striking contrast to the small figure of Louisa. But as his young sister planted her hands on Frederic's shoulders to keep his balance, Henry felt something inside him shift. Perhaps he had been hasty and uncivilized. Perhaps he had imagined a violent sexual assault that never occurred. Perhaps he had been wrong.

"Elaine!" Louisa called, waving her arms about. "Would you come here please?"

Sensing the concern in her voice, Elaine tucked a black lock behind her ear and flitted her eyes across the way to take in the sight of Louisa. Hopeful, she lifted her hand to shield the sunlight from her face and then glanced back at Henry with a look of admonishment.

"Yes!" Elaine shouted back. "Will you be all right alone for a moment, Henry?"

"Yes." Henry slumped against the trunk of the tree and gestured his hand. "Go to her, Elaine. It appears I have some matters to sort through on my own."

"All right." Elaine leaned down and left a kiss on Henry's cheek. "I shall return."

As Elaine sprinted across the sand, Henry reclined against the tree and clumped his fingers through the sand. He cocked his head to the side and strained to listen once Elaine reached Louisa and Frederic. Somehow, Louisa beamed anew like a glowing ray of sunlight.

"Oh, Elaine." Louisa pulled her sister-in-law into her arms and gave her a tight squeeze. "We thought you were both dead." She closed her eyes and breathed a sigh of relief.

"What on earth gave you that idea?" Elaine took a step back to hold Louisa at arm's length. Even though Frederic remained by her side, Elaine hardly felt in the way.

"Judas," Louisa replied, swaying her posture as the wind cut through her hair.

Gazing out at the horizon, Elaine mulled over the matter and bit her lip.

"You cannot imagine the terrible things he has done to me," Louisa said.

Elaine begged to differ. "I assure you that I can," she returned.

"You have no idea how long we have been searching for you, Elaine." Louisa placed her balance on one foot and then the other, bouncing back and forth. "I thought I might never see either of you again. Thank God for Frederic."

Elaine lifted her chin and glanced over at the man. He was no more than a stranger to her.

Upon first sight, Elaine had loathed the captor. For he had been the one to assist Judas and even drag poor Louisa into the jungle to treat her in whatever way he wished.

But Louisa hardly seemed frightened of Frederic now. Elaine recognized the rushing blood against the young girl's cheeks as a sign of mutual friendship and attraction. Perhaps Frederic had never harmed her. Perhaps he had saved her. Perhaps he had rescued her.

With the way Louisa kept referring to the pair as we, Elaine understood that an irreprehensible bond had formed between them. Perhaps Frederic deserved not punishment but praise. After all, he could be the sole reason why dear Louisa was still alive.

"I would like to thank you, sir, for saving the life of my sister." Elaine held her hand out for Frederic to shake. "You have done a great service to us all. I can never thank you enough."

Still off kilter, Frederic hardly cracked a smile. But he took Elaine's hand when she offered it, not wanting to be rude. "It was no problem at all, I can assure you."

"Well, I would like to apologize on behalf of my husband." Elaine looked back over her shoulder at Henry. "After the way you dragged

Louisa off, I am sure you can imagine his thoughts. To be honest, I thought the same."

Frederic cleared his throat and swallowed. "I won't let anyone harm Louisa." Draping a protective arm around her shoulders, he pulled Louisa close and she took his hand.

Such a tender touch of affection mesmerized Elaine. Her lively green eyes dropped down to watch the way Frederic tangled his fingers through Louisa's. Somehow, amid the strife, violence and danger, the couple had undoubtedly found love. How could Elaine condemn the act? It was the same method that had led her to a happy life with Henry.

"I am pleased to hear that." Elaine regarded Frederic and Louisa with a subtle smirk.

"Have you seen Judas?" Louisa grabbed Elaine's arm. "He keeps coming after me. One night he chased us through the forest with a pistol. Then he tied me to a tree, covered my clothes in blood and left me for dead. I was nearly eaten alive by a crocodile."

Elaine widened her eyes and parted her lips. "Judas shot Henry."

Louisa took a breath and held a hand to her chest. "Is he very badly hurt?"

"I have removed the bullet and cleaned the wound," Elaine answered. "If not for the volcano, Judas would have done much worse. He has already shoved Henry off a cliff. We are lucky that Henry survived." Warm air passed through her

34

lips. "He is lucky to be alive."

"Until Judas is dead, we are all at risk," was Frederic's earnest reply.

"Yes." Elaine nodded in agreement. "Please. Come meet my husband, Henry."

Chapter 5

Perhaps we should stay inland," Frederic suggested. "Judas will find us here."

Henry scowled and set his golden glower on the speaker. "He will find you anywhere."

Stiffening at the response, Frederic fluttered his dark lashes and regarded Henry affably. Despite a long-winded and highly plausible explanation from his own sister's mouth, Henry had yet to regard Frederic as anything more than a wayward captor. Henry could not picture the very man who had appeared to be Judas's right hand man to suddenly mold into Louisa's knight in shining armor. Apart from truth, reality, and reason, Henry disliked Frederic, because he could not trust him.

"Yes, but we are easier to spot in broad daylight than hidden in the forest. Are we not?"

"Well, you would know now, Mr. Holmes. Wouldn't you?" Henry countered.

Frederic clenched his jaw and smoldered down

at the man in the dirt. While Henry was the younger of the two, he would sooner die than take orders from a scoundrel turned hero. Henry had seen Frederic take Louisa and drag her off into the jungle. It was an image that would never sit well with Henry, because it was one that he could never forget.

"You think my experience as a hunter provides no advantage to us?" Frederic asked.

"I am still trying to reconcile with the absurd possibility that you would provide advantage to any of us," Henry fired back. "You are a liar and a thief. You stole my sister."

"Henry," Louisa butted in. "If you could only open your mind and see that you are not describing Frederic at all. He has saved my life numerous times on this island."

Henry rolled his eyes in a seething rage, his blood boiling hot.

"I would be dead if it weren't for him," Louisa went on. "Can't you see?"

"Can you see, Louisa?" Henry tossed the question back at her. "You are trusting a man who helped Judas capture you and bring all of us here to this godforsaken place."

Perplexed with doubt, Louisa furrowed her brow and began to wonder.

"We have been taken away from New York and brought here to die," Henry proclaimed. "And that man." Henry lifted a finger and pointed it at Frederic. "The one you claim to love. He is responsible for it all. His kindness has not been brought about by sympathy, but guilt." Henry watched Frederic with a smoldering gleam in his eyes.

"Henry, you must think about this reasonably," Elaine remarked.

"I have thought of it reasonably, my darling." Henry kept Frederic pinned to the sand before him with a threatening glower. "Reasonable is the only thing I am being right now."

Elaine threaded her fingers through her hair in frustration and exhaled.

"But, Henry," Louisa piped up, her voice a breathy, shaky sigh. "I love him."

Narrowing his eyes in disapproval, Henry looked from Louisa to Frederic and then back again. "You love him?"

Henry had heard as much from Elaine, but failed to believe her at the time. Could it be true? That his innocent little sister had fallen for the guilty man in the wild? Perhaps it was easy to believe. After all, Louisa had also expressed similar regard for Judas. Her feelings may have been untainted and true, but they were not good. Loving a man like Frederic or Judas was quite simply dangerous.

"Yes," Louisa cooed, weaving her fingers through Frederic's once she took his hand. "We are in love, Henry. It happened in the forest. Frederic loves me, too."

At the sight of their fingers interlocking, Henry

leapt up and tackled Frederic to the ground. "She is young and naïve," he growled. "And you touched her!"

"No! Henry! Please. Stop!" Louisa reached out, but Elaine held her back.

"I never harmed her," Frederic explained. "But I do love her."

Henry had his hands wrapped around Frederic's throat, but something in the man's silvery gray eyes made him stop. As much as Henry wanted to pummel Frederic into the ground, how could he take away Louisa's only source of joy? If he were lying, surely Louisa would say so now that she had been reunited with family. So why had she failed to utter a single word of his hostile treatment towards her? Was it because a violent attack had never occurred? Because Frederic had never violated or touched or harmed her?

Had Frederic been telling the truth? That he truly loved her?

As honesty flooded through him, Henry sat back on his knees and released Frederic. He looked over the man's body and observed the fresh marks he had left on his neck. Perhaps malice and vengeance for Judas had clung together and swirled through him.

Henry was desperate for revenge, desperate and bloodthirsty. Perhaps the evil of the jungle had crept into the veins beneath his skin. He was not the same man.

"I am sorry I struck you," Henry muttered, though he failed to make eye contact with Frederic. "Forgive me." He rose and hobbled towards the shade tree. "Forgive me."

Frederic lay on the flat of his back in the sand, still panting for air. Slowly but surely, Henry limped his way farther down the island, to the place where the shack had once been.

"I must go to him," Elaine said. "Look over Frederic, will you?"

Louisa nodded and watched Elaine trudge after her brother. The sun was setting in the distance, streams of red and pink blending beneath the cool blue water. As a shudder drifted through her, Louisa knelt down in the sand to care for Frederic.

But then she paused to look back over her shoulder at her brother across the way. Despite her reluctance to admit it, the truth was startlingly clear.

Something was terribly wrong with Henry.

Chapter 6

The moon hung pearly white over a flat tapestry of black as waves crashed against the shoreline. Henry rested beneath the shelter of two beach trees just past the border dividing the jungle from the sand. After setting his nose, Elaine had sat with him for hours in the hope of persuading Henry to forgive Frederic and accept him as a member of the island.

But Henry remained quiet and apathetic, crossing his arms over his chest in resentment. As Elaine left his side to join Louisa by the fire, Henry glowered at Frederic in the distance. He had been fooled, tricked, and betrayed by men in the past who were just like him. Frederic associated with pillagers and pirates. There was no change of heart.

Needing a break from Henry, Elaine reached Louisa and settled down beside her in the sand. Frederic had speared fish earlier in the evening and steamed them over the fire for everyone to eat. As Louisa handed Elaine a piece of meat, she took it with delight and scarfed down the heavenly substance. Elaine could not remember the last time she and Henry had consumed a proper meal, hardly scraping by on coconut milk and berries.

"This is wonderful, Frederic," Elaine crooned, sinking her teeth through the flesh.

He smiled at her from across the flames, his knees tucked into his chest as his arms dangled over his legs. Aware of the awkward tension in the atmosphere, Frederic glanced several hundred feet away and caught Henry's stern, aggressive gaze. There was anger in his light, golden eyes for the transgressions of Frederic's past.

But Frederic had no way of traveling back in time and leaving Louisa untouched. If he had not taken her, they never would have met, much less fallen in love on the island. Yet Frederic knew Henry would not accept the fault of fate or destiny. The fault of Louisa's kidnapping rested on Frederic's shoulders, and so must the punishment as well.

"Perhaps you should speak to my brother, Frederic." Louisa placed her hand on his shoulder and squeezed the tensing muscle there. "Surely, he has calmed down by now."

With a reluctant sigh, Frederic nodded his head and went to stand. He had figured as much while Louisa and Elaine sat there eating the fish he had caught for them. Dinner had been an attempt to restore trust with Elaine and establish it with

Henry. Yet Henry kept his distance and refused to eat, revealing how little trust he had in Frederic.

"Keep the fire low," Frederic recommended. "Wouldn't want to alert Judas."

"Yes, my love." Louisa lifted her head up as Frederic leaned down to gift a kiss on her cheek. "Don't let him be too harsh on you. He doesn't understand. You have done nothing wrong."

Frederic wasn't so sure that he agreed with that, but he nodded anyway and let go of her hand. Surprised by Louisa's term of affection, Elaine darted her eyes between the pair with a smirk on her face. When Frederic walked away and headed towards Henry, he heard the sound of Elaine whispering in Louisa's ear and wondered what she had to say about him.

His arms hung limply by his sides on the journey to see Henry beneath the beach trees. Frederic may have been nearly five years older, yet Henry startled him with the sheer look of hatred in his eyes. With no clue how to atone for his sins, Frederic placed one hand in his pocket and the other against one of the trees when he arrived.

"Why have you come?" Henry began. "You wish to speak to me?"

Frederic took an immediate step back and looked out at the inky blue waves as they came crashing against the shore. "What can I do?" he asked. "How can I prove my worth?" Desperate to fix things, Frederic glanced over at Henry in a silent plea.

Henry scoffed at the remark and shook his head. "You can't."

Frederic dug his heel into the sand and quirked his mouth to the side.

"I am never going to accept you," Henry confessed. "You have aided the man who has nearly taken everything from me. You stole my sister and brought her here."

"Yes, but I only did those things because—"

Henry held a hand up and silenced him. Then he nodded towards the women he loved as they chatted by the fire. "Do you love her?" His golden gaze drifted from Elaine to Louisa.

Frederic looked at the blonde beauty from afar, hardly able to believe that she loved him. Her presence in his life was like a dream come true, one that he had never dared aspire to. Louisa was good and innocent, sweet and beautiful, precious and kind. While he didn't deserve her, he couldn't deny wanting to please her for the rest of his life.

"Yes," Frederic answered, his eyes on Louisa. "I do. I love her."

Henry pressed his back against the trunk of the tree and adjusted his posture to better suit his injured leg. "Would you mind sitting up later? For the first watch?"

Perking his ears up, Frederic turned back to Henry in relief. "Not at all."

If Frederic could prove to Henry that he only wanted to help, perhaps Henry would move past disagreements of the past. Frederic loved Louisa and wanted to keep her safe. Perhaps pleasing her elder brother would be the only way how.

"Good." Henry pressed his palm into the sand and struggled to stand, gritting his teeth with the pain of forced effort.

"Let me help you." Frederic reached out a hand and clasped Henry's shoulder.

"No!" Henry withdrew immediately and stumbled backward, yet regained his bearings by leaning into the tree. "Please tell my wife that I have lain down to rest."

"Yes, Henry." Frederic lingered nearby. "I will tell her."

Once Frederic watched Henry go, he had no clue whether they had reached an agreement or not. Surely, he would have time to redeem himself, even though he had caused Louisa no harm on the island. If anything, he had been her sole source of protection, saving her life countless times from falling trees, wild beasts and even Judas. But no matter how honorable the rescue may sound, there was no appeasing Henry tonight.

On his trek back to the fire, Frederic hung his head and sighed. How could a demon ever fall in love with an angel? Frederic had worked for the devil, but Louisa had pulled him into the light. Regardless, his troubled past was the only thing Henry was going to go by.

Chapter 7

Elaine slowly breathed in and out, contently
nestled in her husband's arms. As she drifted
off with her head on his chest, Henry was wide
awake, his glowing eyes readily fixed on Frederic's
silhouette in the distance. Louisa came running up
to Frederic and leapt into his arms, while Henry
gritted his teeth and restrained himself from
attacking at the sight.

"Lie down with me, Frederic." Louisa took his
hands and peered up at him with those sweet blue
eyes. "I am ready for bed." She fluttered her
lashes and grinned.

Frederic chuckled in the dark, amused at her
temperament. "But we have no bed."

Pulling him towards her, Louisa leaned up on
the tips of her toes and whispered in his ear.
"Then let's make one." She pressed a delicate kiss
to his cheek and then ran her fingers through his
beard, reveling in the rough, bristly texture.

"Your brother has asked me to stand guard for

the night," he revealed.

Disliking Henry's orders, Louisa pinned her eyebrows together as the angelic grin fled from her face. "But you must sleep, Frederic. The whole night? That is—"

"Your brother has been shot, Louisa." He brushed his thumb along the side of her face. "Time will tell if Elaine has dressed the wound properly."

Louisa turned her cheek into the palm of his hand and frowned in disappointment.

"Henry deserves a good night's rest," Frederic murmured, half regretting his decision to leave Louisa to sleep alone when he had been her constant comfort.

"So do you." Louisa stepped close enough to wrap her arm around his waist.

But Frederic darted his eyes up at the sight of Henry watching them in the distance. Even from afar, he caught the brutal warning piercing the edge of Henry's aura.

"Why don't you join your brother and Elaine?" Frederic withdrew his hand from Louisa's cheek and forced a sliver of space between them. "So you won't be cold."

Absorbing the bitter sting of rejection, Louisa uncoiled her arm from his body and scanned his face with careful concern. "If that is what you wish," she whispered.

"It is." Frederic stared into her bright blue eyes. "Go on now."

Confused and hurt, Louisa stepped backwards in the sand. "Good night, Frederic."

"Good night, dear Louisa." Frederic sank his teeth into his lower lip and balled his hand into a fist at his side the moment she began walking away.

Isolated from the group, Frederic looked on as Louisa approached Henry and Elaine. She hardly said a word to her brother, though Frederic was too far to decipher what. When Louisa lay down on the other side of Elaine, Henry stared at the back of her head for a very long time. By the time she drifted off, he could not contain his silence any longer.

Leaving Elaine and Louisa to dream, Henry rose to his feet and set his hand along the tree to catch his balance. Then he kept his eyes down and limped across the sand until he reached Frederic several hundred yards away. Astounded at his approach, Frederic lowered his head with a welcome nod and swallowed.

"Have you spotted anyone yet?" Henry asked.

"No. Not yet. We should be safe for the night," Frederic predicted.

Despite Henry's six foot stature, Frederic stood nearly three to four inches taller than him. So Henry lifted his head to gaze up at the man who could have killed him with his bare hands if he so desired. "If you love Louisa, you must want what is best for her."

"Why yes," Frederic agreed, searching Henry's

face. "Of course."

"Now that Elaine and I are here, Louisa will be safe again."

"She was safe before," Frederic reasoned. "I kept her safe. I keep her safe."

The corner of Henry's mouth lifted into a patronizing smile. "She was safe before you kidnapped her," he stated. "She would have been safe if you had left her alone in New York. My wife lived on this island as a child, and I have lived here with her."

Frederic closed his mouth and nodded to show that he was listening.

"We can survive. We can protect Louisa. Without you."

Frederic cocked his head to the side as warmth flowed through his body. Reality set in, for Frederic inherently understood the meaning of Henry's words.

"You want me to leave?" Frederic posed. "Abandon Louisa?"

Henry lifted a finger in disagreement. "You won't be abandoning her. Elaine and I are perfectly capable of taking care of Louisa on our own. To be frank, I just don't trust you."

Frederic placed his hands on his hips. "I understand how you feel. Truly, I do but—"

"You are no good for her, Frederic," Henry bluntly stated. "Our father is dead, and I am the man in her life now. I do not approve of the relationship. You will stay away from her."

Surging with disappointment, Frederic scratched his chin and looked over at the distant stretch of sand where Louisa slept. "You plan to keep us apart," he said.

"If our father were alive, he would do the same for her." Henry followed Frederic's line of sight and patted him on the shoulder. "You must know in your heart that it would never work between the two of you. She is still a child, and you are older than I am."

"But Henry, I know you would be better off if I were here." Frederic motioned towards the ground and stared at the cloth tightly wrapped around Henry's leg. "You have been shot. You are wounded. And you know Judas is still lurking in the forest."

"Precisely," Henry noted. "How do I know you aren't spying on all of us on his behalf right now? You've followed his orders before. I've seen you do it."

Frederic stole a glance of sleeping Louisa in the dark and looked out at the sea.

"Stay the night," Henry requested. "But I want you gone by morning."

When Henry turned on his heel to leave, Frederic grabbed his arm. "But Henry. Please," he begged, furrowing his brow in suffering. "I love her."

Henry took a deep breath and shifted to face Frederic. "Then you will let her go."

Utterly lifeless, Frederic stood stock still as

Henry left him alone and made his way back to Elaine and Louisa. After Henry took a seat in the sand and Elaine placed her head in his lap, Frederic peered across the distance at Louisa asleep on the ground. He mashed his lips together and winced, fighting the urge to walk over and convince her to run away with him into the woods. Surely, she would say yes. But he couldn't bring himself to do it.

So Frederic took a step back as thriving hot tears stung his eyes. With one long stride after the next, he walked across the sand and approached the shoreline. Then he sat down in the wet mud and let the waves crash over him, mournfully gazing up at the moon.

Chapter 8

Louisa startled awake with a kick, reaching out for the warmth of a man who wasn't there. She sat up and gazed out at the sea to find Henry and Elaine sitting along the shoreline. Water washed over their feet with the surge of each oncoming wave.

Peering up at the rising sun, Louisa lifted her hand to block out the light. Since Elaine had always been Henry's greatest distraction, Louisa recognized her golden moment of opportunity and capitalized on it. She hurried to her feet and ran along the border of the jungle, digging up loose sand with every step. But when Louisa reached the spot where Frederic had stood guard last night, he was gone.

"Frederic?" Louisa called, turning about in a half circle. "Frederic, where are you?"

There was nothing more than the pleasant sound of birds chirping and a heavenly breeze throughout the forest. Too cautious to walk into the woods alone, Louisa ambled towards the edge and called out his name again. But there was no reply.

Impatient to see Frederic, Louisa turned around and skipped across the sand until she reached Henry and Elaine. "Have either of you seen Frederic this morning?" she asked.

"No, Louisa. I haven't," Elaine replied. "Henry, have you seen Frederic?"

Too ashamed to face her, Henry bowed his head and folded his hands together. Either of the women might have thought he was praying if his brown eyes weren't flitting over the ocean. Without a word, Henry moistened his lower lip and kept to himself.

"I'm sorry, Louisa." Elaine offered an empathetic shrug. "I don't know where he is."

"Perhaps he decided what was best," Henry grumbled. He cleared his throat and finished, "What was best for you I mean, considering the circumstances."

Louisa felt dizzy and sick, as if the whole world were about to fall away beneath her feet, as if the island were a false reality, as if she were merely tangled up in a lucid dream.

"Henry, you didn't," she hesitated, noticing his indifference towards her. Tears threatened to fill her eyes as she began to back away from him. "Henry, you wouldn't."

"I was only thinking of you," Henry explained. "Of what was best for you. Of what Father would do." He looked over his shoulder at her, never intending to come across so harshly. "You must know that men like Frederic Holmes are a dime a dozen."

"No," Louisa cried, dabbing at the flood of hot tears running down her face. "NO!" She turned and ran for the jungle, desperate to catch Frederic and get as far away from Henry as possible.

"Louisa! Wait!" Henry shouted after her.

As he shifted to rise to his feet, Elaine grabbed his arm and stopped him. "Let her go, Henry," she declared. "Is it true? Did you ask Frederic to leave?"

Sighing aloud, Henry sat back down in the sand and gazed out at the horizon.

"Henry!" Elaine slapped his arm and could care less if it stung.

But Henry failed to flinch, knowing that her admonishment was one he deserved. "Listen, Elaine. I was only doing what was best for her. Louisa is no more than a child, and there is no good in her daydreaming about that man. It's how Father would have wanted it."

Elaine threaded her fingers through her hair and groaned. "Henry, what on earth is the matter with you? Do you know why Frederic even captured Louisa in the first place?"

"Yes, because he is a despicable man who can't be trusted," he spat back.

"No." Placing her palm against his arm, Elaine fluttered her lashes and searched every inch of

Henry's hard face. Even when he failed to glance her way. "Judas has taken Frederic's father prisoner. If Frederic does as he says for one year, then his father will go free."

Henry mulled over the matter and tilted his head to the side. As he stroked his jawline, Henry mused, "Perhaps that is what he told Louisa to make her believe him, to make her trust him."

"Henry, for once in your life, could you at least try to give someone else the benefit of the doubt?" Elaine rose to her feet. "For goodness sake, have some compassion."

"I have no compassion for men who associate themselves with the likes of Judas. If you weren't so set on Louisa having her way, you would see that I am right, Elaine."

Turning towards him with a scowl on her face, Elaine glared at the back of Henry's head and set her hands on her hips. "You could have just destroyed any chance that girl might ever have of happiness on this island. Did you ever stop to think of that?"

Henry chewed at the inside of his cheek as her words reverberated through him. Digging his elbows into the sand, Henry reclined back and relished the sea breeze. As salt drifted through the air, he came to his senses and looked back. "Elaine!"

But she ignored him and trudged through the sand, swinging her arms from side to side. Her lustrous black locks blew through the wind, matching the rhythm of her hips as she swayed them back and forth. Henry sat there in the sand and watched her go, unable to grasp how he had managed to get the two remaining women in his life angry with him at the same time.

* * *

Trees rushed past Louisa in a blur as she plunged ahead like a lion chasing prey. A wayward branch snagged the hem of her dress, and Louisa tumbled backwards. Out of breath, she steadied herself once she managed to stand on two feet, perspiring with sweat.

"Frederic!" she cried out. While it may not have been wise to shout his name in the wilderness, where Judas would never be one to turn a deaf ear, she could not help it.

Silence resumed in between intervals of her yelling his name. Eventually, she turned quiet and continued her journey into the jungle, willing to reach the deepest parts if she had to. If Frederic was truly gone, then she had to find a way to bring him back.

Leaping across a cool brook, Louisa knelt down once she reached the other side. She dipped her hands into the water and took a refreshing drink, then splashed the remaining liquid all over her face and neck. When she lifted her head, the sun beat down from its throne in the sky, blistering with heat at high noon.

While she must have spent hours in the

jungle, Louisa never complained on her mission to find Frederic. She searched high and low until her palms were dripping with sweat and the soles of her feet were calloused and tender. She trekked onward until her back ached, placing her hands along the area of tension. Despite her struggle, Frederic was worth every moment of the pain. She would not live without seeing him again. If Frederic planned to leave the Rochester clan, he could at least have the decency to say goodbye.

When it seemed that all was lost, Louisa arrived at the candy colored spring where the panther had led them yesterday. Frederic crouched down before the water on one knee, gazing out into oblivion. Perhaps he was contemplating the future safety of the treasure? Or maybe he had returned to the last place where Louisa had told him that she loved him.

"Frederic," Louisa quietly uttered, slowing her footsteps once she reached him.

At the sound of her voice, he bolted into an upright position and looked her over. Louisa had been trampling through the forest and made a mess of her clothes. In all honesty, her dress had not been clean since Judas ruined the fabric with blood stains.

"Hello, Louisa." His Adam's apple bobbed as he swallowed, turning away.

"Where are you going?" She approached Frederic from behind and came close enough to him without touching. "Why did you leave?"

Unaccustomed to his silence, Louisa pressed further and asked, "Were you really going to leave without saying goodbye?"

Frederic bit down on his tongue and hoped that it bled. He stood with his back to her and felt the warmth of her body all around him. If he walked away now, perhaps it might soften the blow. But how could he leave when the one he desired most was right here?

"Frederic?" Louisa touched his shoulder but he remained frozen. "Speak to me."

He turned back at her command and got in her face. "Speak to you? About what?"

Caught off guard, Louisa held her own and gazed into his murky gray eyes. They were far from silver today, like stormy clouds or molten metal instead. "I thought that—"

"You thought what, Louisa?" he interrupted, rebuking her. "That we would ride off into the sunset like some storybook ending from one of your fairytales?"

"Whoever said I had a fairytale?" Louisa responded, taking offense.

"You're a girl from the city." He knocked her shoulder as he brushed by and took to pacing in a slow circle. "Of course you want a fairytale. And I'm no prince."

Blinking several times, Louisa took a step forward, but he kept putting distance between them. "What are you talking about? You think I concern myself with that?"

Frederic planted his hands on his hips and lingered exceptionally close for a change. "Just face it, Louisa." He stood no more than an inch from her and lowered his voice, "I'm not good enough for you. I was born a street rat, girl. No fine mansion and crystal chandeliers. I am a thief, and that is all I will ever be."

"Frederic," Louisa whimpered, her lower lip trembling. "Don't say that."

"Why shouldn't I say it?" He waved his arm about in frustration. "It's the truth."

Louisa scanned his beautiful face, ruggedly handsome and defiant. She didn't care if he was a reformed criminal. She didn't care if he was fourteen years her junior. She only cared that she loved him. Because that was all that mattered.

"What did my brother say to you?" Louisa let out a shaky breath and quivered.

Frederic struggled for air, his chest rising and falling at the scorching heat between them. How desperately he wanted to reach out and place his hand on her warm neck and feel the burning fire beneath her skin. But that would only result in his eventual torture, so he kept to himself.

"Nothing," Frederic hissed. "I made this decision myself."

Narrowing her eyes, Louisa held her chin high and glowered up at him. "You're lying."

"Look!" Frederic took a step forward and held his hand in the air, as if he were struggling to resist the alluring beauty of her aura. "I don't want you anymore."

Seamlessly unmoved, Louisa stared straight into his eyes without blinking.

"I am a grown man, Louisa." He scanned her body from head to toe, taking in the curves of her figure. "And you are just a silly little girl."

"Is that so?" Louisa clutched her elbows and regarded him with censure.

"Yes," Frederic rasped, unable to reckon why he could never seem to catch his breath around her. Her mere presence sucked it right out of him, like a wind tunnel in a storm.

"You don't want me anymore?" She spoke from a small, still place of doubt.

Frederic slid his tongue along the front of his teeth and moistened his lips before biting down. With the clench of his jaw, he held her forceful gaze and replied, "No."

"You don't want to hold me?" she tested him. "You don't want to touch me?" Louisa pressed her palm against his beating heart and rubbed the fabric over his chest.

"Louisa," he scolded, darting his eyes down to her hand.

Angry and hurt, Louisa ripped her hand away and glared into his steely gray eyes. When tears flooded her vision, sadness drifted across Frederic's face, reshaping his features into an expression of loss and regret. He longed to apologize, reach out and take her hand, tell her how sorry he was. But that would only prolong the pain of the inevitable break.

Louisa moved closer to his body until there wasn't a sliver of space left between them. Then she peered up into his eyes and set her bright blue ones on him. "If you truly don't want me anymore, then why don't you kiss me? What better way to prove it?"

Ready to accept her challenge, Frederic ground his teeth together and gazed down at her sweet warm lips. She had brought up the challenge to push and test him, because she knew he could not turn her away. Her love was something he had never been able to resist.

"All right, then." Frederic dragged each of his thumbs against his fingertips. "A goodbye kiss? Is that what you want?" He inhaled her scent and hadn't expected the pain that flooded his body at the thought of never tasting her again.

"No." Louisa grabbed the skirt of her gown and turned on her heel, nearly collapsing to the ground from spinning in a circle so fast. She wanted to witness how unwilling he truly was to give her up, how much of a struggle it would be, how much he wanted her to stay.

Alive with the thrill of a chase, Frederic went after Louisa and clasped her arm. As he turned her small body back into his embrace, Louisa attempted to resist him and a subtle whimper escaped her mouth. Not giving her the chance to deny him, Frederic clamped his hand around Louisa's waist and brought his mouth to hers.

At first Louisa tried to fight him off, but the tingling shivers that traveled down her spine put all of that to rest. Frederic pulled her body closer and moved his mouth against hers, sucking in her every breath. Cooing in response, Louisa's hands landed on his chest as she relaxed into his arms and let him touch her in every which way he allowed.

Frederic paused for breath and then met her lips with a soul-stirring kiss, hoping that the sensation traveled all the way to her knees. Once he dragged his teeth over her lower lip and let go, Louisa stood with her eyes closed and her cheeks on fire. Unwilling to give him up, she stepped into him and planted her mouth on his once more. She wanted him to feel all the many things he was making her feel, in the feeble hope of keeping him.

Despite his internal battle, Frederic squeezed Louisa's wrists and stepped back until they broke apart. When he regarded her with apathy, Louisa glanced up at him with angry tears in her eyes. He placed her hands by her sides and let go. It was the last time they would ever touch, the last time he would ever see dear, sweet Louisa again.

"I must go," Frederic mumbled, tearing his gaze away from the darling girl.

"Don't leave me!" Louisa cried. "You said you would never leave me." She staggered forward and clutched his forearm. "You said you would protect me. You promised."

Ashamed, Frederic withdrew from her grasp and stared at the forest beneath his feet.

When Louisa understood that he had no intention of ever speaking to her again, she slammed her hands against his chest until he stumbled backwards. It was a final attempt to provoke him into changing his mind, as well as one last chance to touch him again.

"Goodbye, Mr. Holmes." Louisa stole a glance of his gray eyes and amber locks before turning on her heel and running through the forest. She committed his face to memory.

As she fled into the distance, Frederic clenched his jaw and fumed with rage. When the silhouette of her long blonde hair diminished into the light, he balled up his fist and slammed it into a tree. Bruising pain rocked through his body as he extended his fingers and looked down at the damage he had done. Nothing in comparison to separation from the love of his life. That girl. The girl. His only girl.

Frederic looked off for Louisa, but she was gone.

He hoped he had not caused her pain.

Chapter 9

For the longest time, Louisa lay down in the jungle and cried. She could hardly believe that the same forest where he had confessed his love for her was the same one where he had confessed that he never wished to see her again. The pain ripped through her like a knife in the chest. How could he abandon her at a time like this? While she had been reunited with her family, they could never provide the comfort of a man like Frederic.

Gathering her strength, Louisa dried her eyes and rose to her feet. Then she wiped her hands on her dress and moved one foot in front of the other, though it hardly felt like she was moving at all. She kept thinking that Frederic was standing right behind her. That all she had to do was simply turn around and there he would be.

Desperate, she paused and looked back over her shoulder, but no one was there.

Once Louisa reached the edge of the jungle, she stepped into the sand and walked across the beach. Henry and Elaine were eating beneath the shelter of a few beach trees. While Louisa could have shown her anger and lashed out at Henry, she no longer had the strength to.

"Hello, Louisa. Are you all right?" Elaine set those striking green eyes on Louisa and offered an expression of sorrow and sympathy. "I was worried about you."

Louisa took a seat beside Elaine and glared at Henry. "Frederic has left."

"Oh?" Elaine sipped at coconut milk from its shell. "Where has he gone?"

Henry reclined on his elbow and perked his ears up. He had yet to acknowledge Louisa or even speak a word. Deep down, Henry was wrestling with the probability that he should have kept Frederic as an ally instead of giving him just cause to become an enemy. The auburn-haired lass loved young Louisa, and that was the protection Henry hoped for.

"I spoke with him in the forest." Louisa lowered her eyes and used her finger to draw pictures in the sand. "He is not the man I thought he was," she confessed.

"Did he harm you?" Henry inquired, tilting his head in her direction.

"If you must ask, no brother, he did not harm me," she fired back.

"We will be better off without him," Henry declared.

"Why?" Louisa snapped. Hot tears resurfaced

against her bright blue eyes.

"He cannot be trusted." Henry kept calm and dared her to cross him.

"Frederic is a tall, strong man," Louisa noted. "He could have provided protection to all of us. Look at you, Henry," she scowled. "You've been shot in the leg and can hardly walk! However would you be able to defend us both?"

"You may hate me now, but I have only done what is best," Henry assured her. "I am thinking of you."

"Thinking of me!" Louisa rose to her feet and jabbed a finger at him. "No, you weren't thinking of me! The only person you were thinking of is yourself!"

Storming off, Louisa fought back the tears and failed to rid the knot of a lump from her throat. She loved her brother, but he had done something so horrendous that it made her hate him. Frederic was her only source of light in the jungle. And now he was gone.

"What of Judas?" Elaine prompted, turning her head to gaze at Henry. "What will you do if he attacks one night? You know he is not dead! You know he is still on the island! I cannot believe you would do something as foolish as drive Frederic away!"

"He can't be trusted, Elaine!" Henry shouted. "How many times do I have to say it?"

"No." Elaine stood with the shake of her head. "You're the one who can't be trusted."

Angry with his bravado, Elaine ran across the sand to join Louisa and talk on the shoreline. How dare Henry place the full weight of decisions on his shoulders! Just because he was the eldest? Just because he was the man? Of every Rochester on the island, he was the one who could hardly walk, the one who had been shot, the one who needed help.

When Elaine reached the ocean, she looked back over her shoulder and let her black hair whip against her face in the wind. She spotted Henry in the distance and glowered before sitting down beside Louisa and touching her arm. At the first sign of comfort, Louisa turned into Elaine's embrace and cried. Elaine hugged her close as she wept, patting her back in an attempt to ease her through the mourning of heartbreak.

Henry bit his lip at the sight of them clinging to one another, as if Louisa could not confide in her own brother. How could it be that his wife and sister were both angry with him when all he had been trying to do was protect them? Unable to bear the tension any longer, Henry got to his feet and limped away. He looked back over his shoulder at Elaine and Louisa one last time. Then he took another step and wandered into the jungle.

They would be better off without him.

* * *

When the pearly moon hung pretty in the

night sky, Louisa lay down in the sand and looked up at the stars. She wished more than anything in the world that Frederic were right here watching them with her. Instead, Elaine approached and took a seat beside her with fruit to eat from the forest. Louisa hunched forward on her elbows and sighed.

"I can't find Henry," Elaine revealed, offering red berries to Louisa.

She tucked a pale blonde lock behind her ear and breathed, "What?"

"Perhaps he is angry with us both. He is the one who should apologize."

Louisa pressed her lips together and listened to the waves crashing nearby, wondering if Henry was off in the jungle sulking, simply because his opinion of Frederic was one she did not agree with. "Where do you believe he has gone?"

Chewing on berries, Elaine kept her head down and sighed. "I don't know."

"Hmm." Louisa settled in the sand and contemplated the matter. "Would you have asked Frederic to leave?" She took a berry from Elaine's palm and popped it into her mouth. "Knowing all that you know now? After everything I have told you?"

Elaine paused and glanced up at Louisa, her appetite suddenly suppressed. "No." She shook her head and looked down as if she were trying to identify every grain of sand. "Especially after everything you have said." She handed the rest of the berries to Louisa and was glad when she accepted them. "Frederic has not harmed you," Elaine noted. "And with Henry wounded, it would have only helped to have another strong man around."

With a slow nod, Louisa nibbled at the berries, taking them in one at a time.

"But, Louisa?"

The young girl turned her head at the sound of her name and stared into the glistening green eyes of her sister-in-law. They held her to the spot, because an inquisition was near.

"When you were with Frederic in the forest," Elaine murmured, sure to hold her gaze without blinking. "Exactly what happened between the two of you? Did he...?"

"No, Elaine!" Louisa shook her head from side to side. She could see now that Henry had labeled Frederic a miscreant based on his past alone. "Of course not. He would never—"

"I just needed to be sure," Elaine explained, patting Louisa on the shoulder. "You must understand that with the two of you alone in the forest, anything could have happened."

"But don't you see, Elaine?" Louisa beamed as her blue eyes brightened. "Frederic could have been wicked, yet he was not. Is that not enough to show what an honorable gentleman he has become? I know of his past, Elaine. But he has moved beyond that."

Elaine bowed her head and listened, her

fingers sifting through the sand.

"Frederic is a good man, Elaine. He told me that he loved me," she confessed.

"Does he?" Elaine countered, only thinking of innocent Louisa and her heart.

"Yes." Louisa gazed up at the moon with a smile. "I believe he does."

"But you believed Judas loved you as well. Did you not?"

Louisa turned her head to Elaine with a piercing gleam in her eyes. For the life of her, she could not understand why Elaine had chosen to play devil's advocate, especially at a time like this. Why must everyone question Frederic? Would it ever stop?

"Yes, but Frederic is different. He is not like that. I would know."

Elaine moved her head, though it was more of a lazy nod.

"Do you remember when we first arrived on the island and you watched him take me away?" Elaine nodded, so Louisa went on. "The moment we were out of sight, he let me go." Louisa spotted a look of surprise in Elaine's eyes. "He took the key from his pocket and unlocked the shackles on my wrists. He let me go, Elaine. He freed me."

"And why would he do that?" Elaine looked off only to gaze right back.

"Because he is a good man." Her heart was beating with every mention of Frederic's existence. "Just because he has done bad things, that does not make him a bad person."

"And while you were in the forest alone together, he never tried to take advantage of you?" Elaine circled back to her previous concern, determined to know the absolute truth.

"He kissed me and held me when I cried," Louisa admitted. "I hardly think that implies taking advantage. It was never that way between us, Elaine. He loves me."

Ready and willing to listen, Elaine threaded her fingers through her jet black hair and exhaled through her nostrils. Somehow, Louisa had made a decent man out of the criminal with no more than her beauty and charm. Could it be that Louisa had been more than atonement for his sins? That he might have shown kindness towards the poor girl, because he had fallen in love with her?

"Stay here, Louisa." Elaine stood up and brushed the sand from her palms. "I must go search for your brother."

"You mean your husband?" Louisa chirped, smiling with elegant sarcasm.

"Yes." Elaine nodded and walked away, while Louisa looked back and watched her go.

It was odd—the way neither were willing to claim Henry as their own—with Elaine calling him Louisa's brother and Louisa calling him Elaine's husband. Perhaps he could never just be called Henry anymore. Was it because his banishment of Frederic had instilled change?

On her own, Louisa pulled her knees into her chest and gazed down at her gown. Her fingers traveled along the fabric as she studied every stain from her time on the island. Blood. Dirt. Grime. There was a mark for every bruise, cut, and scrape. But nothing remained of the damage left behind from her broken heart. Just emotion. Just great feeling. Just the memory of all it was and all it could never be. Regardless of their short-lived romance in the jungle, it had been novel-worthy. Because it had been real.

Catching a sight in the distance, Louisa leaned forward and pinned her brows together. Panic surged through her veins and made her heart skip a beat, her skin prickling with fear. Louisa thought that she must have been imagining things or perhaps losing her mind. So she stayed put, glued to the sandy shore beneath her, for it must have all been a bad dream.

Before long, a gigantic ship reached the shore with fantastic white sails. Curious as ever, her spirits lifted at the sight, because whoever was onboard must have been an angel or a saint. Perhaps Louisa had seen a ghost, because the sight raised the hairs on the back of her neck.

"LOUISA!" A harsh scream rippled and echoed from the jungle.

Turning back, Louisa looked over her shoulder but made out the image of no one. Ignoring the sound, she turned back to the visiting ship as it pulled in alongside La Fleur Noire.

Something tugged at Louisa's heartstrings and attempted to steer her out of harm's way, but she could not look away from the majestic sight before her.

The ship with white sails left her utterly charmed, transfixed, mesmerized.

"LOUISA!" The voice called again, but she gazed straight ahead and widened her eyes in fear. Men were coming off the boat, one by one, practically a legion of soldiers. When someone grabbed her arm, she yelped and her body shook with fear.

The captain of the ship jerked his head at the sound and spotted Louisa and Elaine along the shore. Pulsing with fear, Louisa gasped as every crewman looked over and whistled at the presence of two young women stranded on a deserted island together without a man in sight. Sweat collected at the nape of Elaine's neck, and her mouth had already turned to sandpaper. What a convenient time for Henry and Frederic to leave.

Distinguished by the ruby red feather in his hat, the captain pointed a finger across the way at Louisa and Elaine and five men came racing towards them. Seized by terror, Louisa could not move a muscle, stock still on the ground as her eyes widened in fear. Unwilling to give in so easily, Elaine grabbed her sister-in-law by the elbow and pushed her forward.

"GO, LOUISA!" she shouted. "RUN!"

Elaine pushed the heel of her hand against

Louisa's back as the trembling blonde took off for the jungle. Looking back over her shoulder with caution, Elaine nudged her on and made sure to keep Louisa a few steps ahead of her. But then Louisa's foot twisted in the sand and she stumbled, toppling over on the ground in defeat.

At the first sign of victory, the crewmen charged ahead to claim such a desirable prize after so many lonely nights at sea. Elaine grabbed Louisa's arms with such force that they nearly broke off as she approached the jungle and pushed Louisa across the border where the forest met the sand. Misunderstanding her actions, Louisa gasped at the pain when her body made contact with the hard ground.

Then Elaine took off in the other direction and raced towards the ship. She dodged and weaved, but in the end one of the men tackled her to the ground and pressed the full weight of his body into her. Watching through the trees, Louisa covered her mouth with her hand as tears pooled in her eyes and stung once they drizzled down her cheeks.

"RUN LOUISA!" Elaine screamed, bucking and flailing about. "RUN!"

Every single one of the men refrained from chasing Louisa into the jungle. Instead, they snatched Elaine up off the ground and steered her towards the ship, a man on either side of her clutching an elbow. Recognizing her window of opportunity, Louisa obeyed Elaine and ran for the depths of the forest without looking back.

As her bare feet pounded against the dirt, she failed to understand why not a single man had followed her. Perhaps she had just been lucky. Elaine was her saving grace, a guardian angel if she had ever had one. There was no doubt Louisa owed Elaine her life.

By the time Louisa had plunged far enough to stop for breath, she hunched forward and her knees buckled. With choking sobs, she lay in the forest and prayed to God in heaven above that those men would not do anything to harm Elaine. Despite Louisa's bright blue eyes and golden blonde hair, the men had hardly noticed her.

It seemed like the only one they had been after was Elaine.

Chapter 10

Well lads, what do we have here?" Captain Scarlett snickered.

Elaine fought against the men who brought her onboard the ship with white sails. Once they reached the deck, she slipped against the wet wood and fell on her hip. Wincing in pain, she leaned back and placed a hand against her hipbone, but they merely laughed.

"Ah, come on darlin'. Get up!" A man with black hair and blue eyes grabbed Elaine by the elbow and jerked her to her feet. She detected the subtle twang to his Irish brogue, but every other man around her sounded English, the captain included.

"Hello there." Captain Scarlett inched forward and tilted Elaine's chin up with the slightest twitch of his hand. She bucked against the black-haired man behind her, though he pushed his back into her chest, restraining her further. She fluttered her lashes at the stench of his breath, as his whiskers brushed against her neck. Soon, every man was drawing near.

"She's a pretty lassie. I'll give her that." His chuckle skittered down her back as the roaring laughter of smelly, drunken men reverberated across the ship.

"Silence!" Captain Scarlett raised his hand in the air. "Now, you pretty creature. What is your name?" He lowered his head so she could not escape his gaze at eye level.

Turning her head about, Elaine struggled for air and tried to decide if she should use an alias or not. If she revealed the name Rochester, that could lead back to New York and Henry. So she held her chin high and feigned bravery, settling on her maiden name instead.

"Elaine Carmichael," she muttered, her lip trembling with the sound.

The Irishman behind her twisted his fingers through her hair and tugged. Her head snapped back as he pulled against her locks harder. "She can put up a fight!" he announced, and the entire crew burst into uproarious laughter. Except for Captain Scarlett.

"Connell?" The captain barked, stalking closer. "Ease up on the poor girl, now. Will you?"

Surprised by his compassion for Elaine, Connell released his hold on her neck and backed away. Elaine placed her hand to her throat and took a breath. Her green eyes searched about the ship, bathed in a pool of men and moonlight.

"Well, Ms. Carmichael, my name is Captain Scarlett. These are my men."

Elaine nodded to the group and ignored the ghastly stench.

"We come from London on a mission to seek out new lands." He tucked his thumbs beneath his belt and cleared his throat. "A group of men from New York sailed out about a year ago and only one came back alive. I believe his name was Henry Rochester."

Her blood turned cold at the sound of her husband's name. They knew who he was. And she had just lied to them. If she had confessed her connection to the lone survivor, would they have shown preference towards her? Could it have been to her advantage to admit that she was a Rochester?

"Do you know the man?" Captain Scarlett cocked his head to the side as the red feather swayed in his hat. The crewmen formed a circled around them, the current conversation, as well as the woman in it, a spectacle to be seen.

Elaine lifted her eyes to meet his and murmured, "No."

Captain Scarlett held a finger to his lips and walked around her figure. "Have you ever heard of him before? Have you ever heard of this man? This Henry Rochester?"

"No," she swallowed, keeping her eyes down. "I have not."

When Captain Scarlett reached her gaze again,

he held his hands behind his back and smiled. "You don't trust me yet, Ms. Carmichael. Do you?"

"How can I?" She shifted her head from side to side to acknowledge the many men onboard. "The moment you arrive, men are chasing after me and grabbing my arm."

"All right." Captain Scarlett clenched his teeth together. "I see."

Connell approached and took her arm. "Shall I have her for the night then?" He shot a sly smirk the captain's way and reveled in the crew's cheering amusement and delight.

"No." Captain Scarlett hovered close enough to get in Connell's face. "You will take your bloody hands off her," he snapped. His piercing gaze seared Connell to the core until he released Elaine and harbored no intention of returning to take her in the night.

Elaine slithered from his grasp the moment he let go and snarled up at Connell. When he winked at her, she felt a shiver creep down her spine. She was going to be sick.

"No one is to lay a hand on this woman! Is that understood?" Captain Scarlett announced.

"Yes, Captain." It was chanted across the ship by every stinking man onboard.

Confused by his protection, Elaine rubbed her hands over her arms and remained calm. There was a chill in the air, a salty night breeze drifting off the sea. When she shivered, Captain Scarlett took off his coat and hung it over her shoulders.

"Thank you." She looked into his eyes with the utmost gratitude, sincere and kind.

"There will be no need for a show tonight, lads," Captain called out. "Continue with your work." When hesitation ensued, he yelled, "Move gentlemen! Now!"

Every strapping young lad returned to his station. Connell touched Elaine's sleeve on his way back and looked over his shoulder at her before walking away. Something about the man made her stomach churn. Perhaps he had only made a scene for show.

"Ms. Carmichael, I would like to speak with you in my cabin."

When Captain Scarlett turned on his heel, Elaine called after him. "If you think I'm going below deck with a stranger I have just met, then you are truly mad."

Pausing in his tracks, Captain Scarlett snorted with a mild laugh. Then he spun around to face her and declared, "I just saved you from a pack of lustful men. Surely you have more thanks to offer me than that." Captain Scarlett grabbed her by the elbow and took off, hurrying to the descending staircase that led to his cabin.

"Let me go!" Elaine protested once they were inside.

But Captain Scarlett shut the door behind them and twisted the lock in place.

"Who are you?" Elaine shouted. "And why are

you really here?"

"Sheer profit, Ms. Carmichael." He walked over to a wooden desk and motioned for her to join him. "Please." His long fingers were scarred and dirty. "Have a seat."

Cautious as ever, Elaine glanced about the room but found nothing unusual. A map pinned to the wall. Jars of miscellaneous sea creatures and shells, some alive. Two handguns on the table by the window.

"Please, Ms. Carmichael." He gestured to an empty chair. "I ask you kindly."

Trudging forward, Elaine slumped down in the seat and wondered if either gun was loaded. If so, she had some form of self-defense, even if she would have preferred another. So she relaxed her shoulders at the idea and turned her full attention over to the captain.

"Someone once told me that there was treasure on this island. Is it true?"

Elaine licked her lower lip and fluttered her lashes. "Perhaps."

"I am here to bargain with Captain William Pierce. Do you know him?"

Elaine stilled at the sound of Judas's false identity and darted her eyes to the floor. There was no denying it now. She had made the truth obvious. "Yes."

"Well, I have given him a head start as he asked." Captain Scarlett pressed the tip of his finger against a piece of parchment on the desk.

"He drew me this map and asked that I come find him. In exchange for treasure, he will receive provisions to last him a lifetime. Food. Clothing. Ammunition. Along with my absolute discretion, of course."

Elaine jammed her fists together when he smiled, and her knuckles cracked.

"In London last summer, Captain Pierce spoke of a woman on this very island." Captain Scarlett looked out the window as the waves jostled the boat. "A woman with hair as black as night and eyes as green as the leaves of a tree."

Elaine watched his eyes drift along her body, taking in the shape of her figure, the long dark locks that hung down her back and glistening green eyes that were utterly striking. Surely, he knew that there had been no mistake. Not many women looked like her.

"He said she was the companion of a jungle cat." Captain Scarlett tilted his head from side to side, weighing her response to the wealth of information. "A panther with a shiny black fur coat and eyes just as green. For a moment, it almost sounded like he believed they were the same. The island girl and the jungle cat. United as one."

Holding her tongue, Elaine set her hands along either arm of her chair. Captain Scarlett folded his fingers together to replicate the act of two becoming one. She felt clammy and sick.

"What do you want from me?" Elaine narrowed her eyes with a hiss.

"I am a trapper, Ms. Carmichael. Do you know what that is?"

She looked down her nose at him and replied, "You take things that don't belong to you and trade them for profit. I don't see how you are any better than a thief."

Captain Scarlett rested his elbows against the table and pressed his folded hands beneath his chin. "Nature is God's gift to man, Elaine. Why would he put something in the world if he did not intend for us to use it, for us to take it? To harness it and extract the value?"

Bold and daring, Elaine stood up and leaned across the table. "A creature in the wild was not placed on this earth for your fortune. You commit murder and seek a profit. That makes you a killer and a thief. What does God think of that?"

"I assume you are the woman Captain Pierce speaks of," he concluded.

"Yes." Elaine leaned back and scoffed, "I am the island girl, and he murdered my jungle cat. He plunged a dagger into her heart and then he carved out her eyes and mailed them to me in a glass jar fill with water and covered in sand. Are you satisfied?"

Captain Scarlett curved his mouth into a crooked smirk. "Not quite."

Glowering down at him, Elaine strutted away and stood before the window.

"I take it that you do not love William, as he led me to believe," Captain Scarlett hinted.

"No, I do not love him," she softly replied. "I loathe him with all of my heart."

Captain Scarlett chuckled at her humor, clapping his hands together in amusement. "I do find you to be remarkably interesting, Ms. Carmichael. I can see now why Captain Pierce has dedicated so much time in returning to you. He appears to be quite taken with you."

"That he does," Elaine agreed. Then she turned to face him and leaned her back against the window. "What purpose do you find in me, Captain?" She held his interested gaze and then uttered, "What would you like for me to do?"

Delighted by her intellect, Captain Scarlett stood up and walked towards her. She did not hold her breath or even flinch, showing no inclination of fear for him. For that reason alone, he admired her and knew that he had found the woman for the job.

"I can earn a great deal more trading pelts of an exotic creature from an exotic land." Captain Scarlett motioned his hand towards the window. "Come into the jungle with me. Help my men find animals the likes of which civilization has never seen before. The rarer the breed the better. Leopards. Panthers. Jaguars. I can make a fortune off a single coat of each."

Elaine gazed through the glass at the moonlight. "And if I help you?" She turned to face him and rubbed the fabric of his jacket where it ghosted across her forearm. "What will I receive in return?"

Captain Scarlett leaned against the wall until he could feel her breath. "From what I gather, Ms. Carmichael, you do not enjoy your affiliation with Captain Pierce. Is that correct?"

"Would I be lying if I said that you were reading too much into our connection?"

"You tell me." He set his sights on her and pulled her gaze inward with a smile.

Blowing him off, Elaine went to turn her back on him and head for the door. She would return his jacket, of course, so long as he let her leave unscathed.

Captain Scarlett grabbed her chin and smoothed his palm along the side of her face, sinking his fingers into her lustrous black locks. "Now I have had just about enough of your behavior, Ms. Carmichael. I could have you slaughtered in an instant by my men at my command."

Elaine peered into his dark eyes as her breathing picked up speed. Blood thrummed violently in her ears, echoing the harsh beating in her chest. Just as her eyes drifted to his open mouth, she recognized that he was standing too close. Much too close.

Seeking to defy him, Elaine reared back and spat in his face. Captain Scarlett wiped the saliva across his cheek and admired her rebellious nature. Finding equal beauty and displeasure in her actions, Captain Scarlett tugged at the back of her head and slammed his lips against hers.

At the unwelcome taste of his mouth, Elaine shoved her palms into his chest until he broke the kiss. Then she lifted her hand in the air and slapped him across the face. Captain Scarlett exhaled at the stinging touch and discovered blood along the fresh cut in his lip.

"If I agree to help you hunt in the wild, you must make it perfectly clear that none of your men are to touch me. You included, Captain." She sighed through her nostrils as her chest rose and fell with the statement, still gasping for air in the cabin.

"William said you did not like to be touched," Captain Scarlett remarked, flicking the dark hair out of his eyes. "Am I to assume that is because of your husband?"

When Elaine's eyes widened with shock, Captain Scarlett sent an evil grin her way.

"Yes, Elaine. William told me all about your dear Henry. Is he still alive?"

Elaine darted her gaze to the ground, for she no longer had the upper hand.

"You cannot keep secrets from me, Ms. Carmichael. I already know them all."

Elaine thought long and hard for a moment. "If I refuse to help you, the life of my husband is at stake? Is that the proposal you are making me?"

He took a long stride towards her and crossed his arms over his chest. "Ignore my wishes, and you'll have made me your enemy. Follow them, and you'll have made me your friend."

Elaine chewed on her lower lip and mulled over the matter. Her thoughts were scattering like the seeds of a dandelion in the wind. "It seems you have left me no choice."

Captain Scarlett placed a hand on her shoulder. "All I ask of you is aid in the jungle while we hunt. If you do as I ask, I guarantee you transport back to America."

"Provided by whom?" she fired back, quick to judge him.

"Why myself, of course!" he taunted. "My men and I will stay no more than a month. If you would like to return home then, I will safely see you to New York."

"All right." Elaine agreed to the deal, solely because she saw no other choice in the mater. "Fine. I agree to your terms. I will help you hunt, just as you have asked."

"Brilliant." Captain Scarlett smiled, and Elaine resented the way it made her cheeks flush with warmth. By the look in his eyes, Captain Scarlett held actual regard for Elaine. Not bound up by greed and selfish desire. Could it be that she had gleaned an ally from an enemy?

"I should like to return to the forest for the night. I promise to—"

"You will do no such thing," Captain Scarlett commanded. "Do you honestly believe I would let you out of my sight?" He touched the soft skin beneath her chin with his finger. "You may see your husband on your journey back to America. In the meantime, you will sleep in here with me. I will be a gentleman enough to lend you my cot."

Seething, Elaine leaned her head back to glower up at him. "May you burn in hell."

"For you, my love?" He warmly caressed her cheek. "I would gladly walk into the flames."

Elaine jerked away from him and peeled his heavy jacket from her shoulders. Once she found his cot along the wall, Elaine lay down and draped his jacket over her torso. Silent tears filled her eyes as she counted lines in the plain wooden board beside her.

Fascinated by such a beautiful creature, Captain Scarlett kept himself awake for most of the night to watch her. She was like a siren lingering at the edge of the bay, crooning soft music to steal his soul away. The truth was, she already had.

Chapter 11

After trekking through the jungle for most of the night, Louisa had almost given up hope. Of finding Henry. Of finding Frederic. Of providing any sort of help for Elaine.

Her strangled scream still echoed overhead, traveling through the air like a blistering cry for help. Stopping for a breath, Louisa rested her hands on her hips and let out a heavy sigh. She felt weak and her shoulders sagged, a testament to her escape from the uninvited.

When a twig snapped beneath her feet, she flinched at the startling sound and tripped. Her body landed on a hard lump of mass. Suddenly, she lay on the flat of her back as a man wrapped his hand around her throat and pinned her to the ground.

Recalling Judas's ever present nature in the forest, Louisa tightened her jaw and winced. Her veins chilled with fear as she felt the weight of his body on top of her. What did he intend to do?

Hit her? Wound her? Ravish her?

"Dear God. Louisa, I'm sorry."

She blinked her eyes open in confusion and found Frederic hovering above her. He leaned back on his knees and helped her sit upright. Bursting with relief, Louisa sailed into his arms and planted her head on his chest. Where it had always belonged.

Frederic circled his palm over Louisa's back and did his best to provide her some comfort. Her body shook with great force as she cried. So he soaked up her warmth and held her close, unable to deny how glad he was that she had come back.

"What is it, dear Louisa? What is the matter?" Frederic set one hand on her shoulder and cradled her face with the other. Though it hadn't even been a day, it felt so good to have the warmth of her skin return. "What are you doing out here in the jungle alone?"

Louisa sat in his lap and curled her hand around the back of his neck. "It's Elaine," she revealed with tears in her eyes. "They have taken Elaine."

Frederic smoothed his thumb across her cheekbone. "Who has?"

"The men on the ship," she sobbed.

"What ship?" Frederic eyed her carefully, his body warming with a sense of unease.

"A ship with white sails." Louisa clung to the collar of Frederic's shirt and carried on, "It came ashore tonight, after we discovered that Henry left."

"What do you mean?" Frederic rubbed her cheek and tucked a fallen lock of blonde hair behind her ear. When she bit her lower lip, Frederic tilted her chin up and stared into her weepy blue eyes.

"Henry left," she sadly remarked. "Henry is gone."

"Gone where?"

Louisa lowered her gaze with a sniffle. "In the forest?" she guessed. "I haven't been able to find him anywhere."

Sensing her panic and fear, Frederic tucked her head beneath his chin and rubbed her back. "We will find him, Louisa," he promised. "I will help you find Henry."

"And what about Elaine?" she quivered. "What about my sister?"

Frederic leaned back and twirled his finger through a lock of her hair. From the start, he had recognized the unbreakable bond between Louisa and Elaine. Though the connection might have only been through marriage, it might as well have been blood.

"We will find her, Louisa. As soon as we find Henry, we will get her back."

Even though Louisa replied with a nod, she doubted her confidence in Frederic. What were the odds that they would be able to find Henry in the forest? He must have been limping around with his bloody gunshot wound. What if they were too late?

"Those men were all around her, Frederic." Her mind flashed back to the sight of poor Elaine as they dragged her away. She had sacrificed her own life, because she knew that Louisa might not be able to handle it. She knew that she was stronger than Louisa, that she could take it more. "What do you think they plan to do with her, Frederic?"

Turning his gaze away, Frederic braided his fingers at the small of her back and cherished the reality that Louisa was safe in his arms. He knew the behaviors of men aboard a ship, so many months spent at sea without the love of a woman, sometimes years. Depriving a man of physical love did strange things to his body, and those urges often resulted in the unfortunate objectification of whichever maiden happened to be close by.

"Do not concern yourself with what could happen, Louisa," Frederic advised.

"Why not?" She treasured the feel of her body encircled in his arms. But her safety was Elaine's torment. "How can I keep from thinking of what they must have done to her?"

Frederic took Louisa's face in his hands and gazed into her eyes with an entrancing force. "Do you believe in God?" He looked to the night sky and then back to her.

"Why yes, of course," she answered, her shaky voice rising with passion and pitch.

"Well, let me tell you a secret, young girl."

Frederic clasped a falling lock of golden blonde and swiped it over her shoulder so he could admire her face. "Something I learned long ago," he revealed, caressing the top of her arm. "God is watching. He sees everything."

"Yes, but how does that help Elaine?" Louisa hung on his every word.

With a weak smile, Frederic scanned her features. Ivory skin. Sapphire eyes. Slender waist. She had every attribute of female youth and beauty that could ever be desired by a man. Yet she was so young, so innocent, so naïve. She had much to learn.

"Everything that you do will come back around eventually," he explained. "It's the law of the world. The law of nature. The law of the jungle. It is real, Louisa. And there is nothing that any man can do to change it."

Louisa leaned in close enough for her breath to rush across his lips. "I hope you are right, my love." She stroked his beard with her finger. "For Elaine's sake, I truly hope you are right."

Unable to hold back with her small body so close, Frederic squeezed her arm and covered her mouth with a tender kiss. She uttered a sweet sigh of contentment when he broke away for air, lovingly running his fingers through her pale flaxen locks. Absorbing his touch, Louisa pushed against Frederic's chest until he lay down on the ground.

Then she snuggled into his comfort and warmth, tangling her leg through both of his. With the back of his head against the forest floor, Frederic secured his hand around her tiny waist and pulled her closer. Louisa put her head on his shoulder and smoothed her hand down the length of his arm.

For just a moment, they lay together in the dark and breathed in the warm evening air. Frederic shut his eyes and pictured her in a soft bed by his side in New York. He refused to let the moment pass him by without imagining it to be more. For it was a fantasy that would never come true.

* * *

Wincing from the pain in his leg, Henry knelt down at the base of a mountainous tree and sucked in a breath of air. The gunshot wound throbbed with rigid tenacity and brunt force, overextending his time since the bandage should have been changed. Had he remained on the beach, surely Elaine would have mended his troubles and catered to his every need, tending to the wound with fresh bandages.

Henry pierced his lower lip with his teeth, turning his head from side to side. He listened for running water, perhaps fortunate enough to happen upon a brook or stream nearby. But he had come across no such luck.

For no more than a minute, he rested against the trunk of the tree and shut his eyes. But then whispers sounded in the night, compelling him to turn rigid and alert. Careful to remain concealed, Henry ducked down behind a gathering of palm fronds and watched whoever was approaching in the forest.

Licking his lips, Henry rested his hand over the dagger along his belt. At the first sight of her swaying blonde hair, Henry reared back and called out to his sister. "Louisa!" he hissed, though she failed to notice. So he stood up and revealed himself. "Louisa!"

Turning around at the sound of her name, Louisa grabbed ahold of Frederic's arm in case danger was near. They both looked back to find Henry placing most of his weight on one foot, while his palm pressed against the bark of the tree. He exhaled aloud and pushed off the tree, limping towards them.

"Henry," Louisa crooned with delight. She rushed over to her brother and wrapped her arms around him. It was a hug rooted in unconditional love. "Wherever have you been?"

Henry planted his hands on her shoulders and left a protective kiss on her forehead. "I am sorry for abandoning you, dear sister. Please forgive me. I wasn't thinking straight."

"You have no idea how happy I am to have found you," she cheered with a smile.

Henry turned his head and nodded over at Frederic. When the latter returned the gesture, a dull silence settled among the trio, reminding them all of the reason Henry had left in the first place. Frederic felt awkward and misplaced now that her brother had come out of hiding. Perhaps Henry was better suited to come to her rescue.

In a surprising gesture, Henry walked around Louisa and extended his hand towards Frederic. "I am sorry for the way I have treated you, sir. Can we forget the matter?"

Louisa cupped her palms over her mouth and held her breath. Happiness surged through her at the sight of the two men in her life making amends. If only Elaine were here to see it.

Frederic lowered his gray eyes and hesitated. Then he quirked his mouth to the side and cleared his throat. "Well, I don't see why not." He took Henry's hand and gave it a firm shake, hoping that the sudden alliance between them would last and hold true.

"Henry, something terrible has happened," Louisa announced.

Furrowing his brow, Henry turned around and regarded her with a frown. "Whatever are you speaking of, Louisa?" Deep down, he didn't want to believe it. Whatever it may be.

"It's Elaine," she inhaled, smoothing out the folds of her gown. "A new ship arrived onshore and the men on it, they came after me. They have taken her, Henry."

Hot air steamed from his nostrils as Henry stewed with a vengeance. Clutching the dagger at his belt, Henry took off and marched through the jungle, despite the biting pain in his leg. How had he been foolish enough to leave her unprotected? How selfish.

"Henry! Where are you going?" Louisa grabbed Frederic's hand and chased after Henry, not wanting him to get too far ahead. "Wait for us!"

"Keep your voice down!" Henry hissed.

Louisa approached with Frederic by her side, and they both skidded to a stop.

Henry paced back and forth, ripping his long fingers through his hair. Frantic and terrified, he nibbled at the inside of his cheek and beat himself up on the inside. If only he had been a kinder brother. If only he had let Frederic stay. If only he had listened to Elaine. She had been angry with him, and he had abandoned her and Louisa to talk and sort through the matter of Frederic on their own. He had abandoned them both.

"Everything is my fault." Henry shook his head and placed his hands on his hips.

"Henry, don't be so hard on yourself," Louisa muttered. "Those men are responsible for taking Elaine."

"But I should have been there!" Henry lifted his finger in the air and then wiped the back of his hand across his mouth. "I should have been there," he repeated, butting the heel of his hand against his forehead.

"Why don't we take a look at the ship?" Frederic suggested. He thought it best to target the problem and find an immediate solution.

Anything else was merely a waste.

Henry took a series of long breaths and nodded. "All right."

Louisa led the way as her two best men kept at her heels, providing protection from all the many dangers of the jungle. When Henry mistook an owl for a predatory creature, he returned his dagger to its sheath and scowled at his ignorance. Frederic kept his distance, though attempted to make friends with Henry. Easier said than done.

"There!" Louisa clung to the skirting of her gown and took off into a full sprint. "I can see the ship straight ahead." She reached the edge of the jungle and knelt down behind the underbrush. "Come, Henry. Look." She pointed and said, "It's the one with white sails."

As Henry crouched down beside Louisa and peered out, Frederic remained in a standing position. Something about the second ship sent a flash of heat beneath his cheeks. Stepping closer, Frederic scratched his head and stroked the beard on his chin.

Why did it look so familiar?

Fuming with rage, Henry rose to dash off, but Frederic drew him back before Henry gave in to hasty revenge. "Calm yourself," Frederic commanded. "Wait a moment."

Louisa reached out to touch her brother's arm, but Henry resisted her affection and put distance between them. When he sank to the ground, Frederic and Louisa shared a look of concern.

"Don't you understand?" Henry complained. "I can't bear it! Knowing that she is trapped in there. Knowing that I disappeared when she needed me most. I just can't!"

Worried that he might break down, Louisa took a seat in the dirt next to Henry and patted him on the back. "We will get her back, Henry. I truly believe it. I wish you would, too."

Henry sniffled and sobbed, dabbing at the sudden tears in his eyes. With a remorseful sigh, Louisa curled her arm around Henry and pulled him into her embrace. As waterworks ensued, Henry placed his head in Louisa's lap and shook with grief.

Clenching his jaw, Frederic turned back and met Louisa's eyes. Henry covered his face with his hands, while Louisa stroked her fingers through his dark shaggy locks in an attempt to calm him down. Taking a shallow breath, Frederic looked back out at the ship in the distance. What bothered him most was the thread of memory in his brain that kept wiggling and writhing about like an earth worm in the ground.

"What did you say again, Louisa?" Frederic snapped his fingers and squatted down behind a tree. "About the man you saw. You said he looked like the captain?"

"Yes." Louisa nodded, her arms securely wound around her brother. "He wore a large black hat with a feather sticking out of it. A dark red feather. Almost the color of blood."

Immediately, all of the pieces clicked into place, and Frederic spun around to gaze back at the ship. With his mouth ajar and his eyes wide open, Frederic stood there gaping in the moonlight. His heart throbbed and his pulse pounded with the rhythm of recognition.

"Frederic?" Louisa regarded him with concern, pinning her blonde eyebrows together. "Frederic, what is it? What do you see?" she asked. "Is someone coming?"

As the shock of the matter seeped in, Frederic squatted down before Louisa and Henry. "I know that ship," he revealed. "I've seen it before."

Louisa shook her head at his words. "What do you mean? Where? How?"

Licking his lips, Frederic looked back over his shoulder. "I've been on it."

Chapter 12

Sunlight filtered in through the window of the captain's cabin as Elaine squirmed on the uncomfortable cot. Trapped in a nightmare, she kicked her way out and woke with a start. When her eyes slammed open, Elaine jolted upright at the sight of Captain Scarlett sitting on the edge of her bed. He looked deeply into her eyes with a lazy smile.

"Good morning, Ms. Carmichael. I trust that you slept well."

Distancing herself from the captain, Elaine clutched the coat over her body and pressed her back into the wall. Her observant eyes darted to the sharp blade and green apple balanced between his hands. As he cut the peel away with his knife, Elaine crossed her arms over her chest in silent reserve.

"Would you like a bite?" Captain Scarlett offered her the circular slice laid across the shiny blade.

Elaine lowered her gaze to the fruit and then returned her eyes to his.

"You're awfully quiet in the morning," he noted. "How does your husband tempt you to speak? It must take a great deal of enticing to get the words out of you."

Elaine blew hot air through her nostrils and held her chin high.

Amused by her silence, Captain Scarlett tore the sliver from the knife with his teeth. He watched her as he ate, wishing she would delight him with her words. He liked the sound of her voice, perhaps because it was the sweetest he had heard since the death of his mother.

"Please say something, Ms. Carmichael. I am rather lonely over here."

"When can I see my husband?" were the first words to leave her mouth.

Captain Scarlett chuckled and slipped another piece of the apple past his lips with the knife. "Your husband," he mused. "Is he the only one you dream about at night?"

"Yes," she swiftly replied. There was no need for hesitation.

"Well." Captain Scarlett munched on the apple. "I would commit murder to have a woman like you dream about me at night. He must be a very lucky man, your husband."

Flooded with emotion, Elaine tossed his coat to the ground and stepped down from the cot. But Captain Scarlett grabbed her arm and held her in place before she could flee.

"Just where do you think you are going?" He levelled his dark eyes at her.

Frozen in place, Elaine bit her tongue and swallowed. In all honesty, she desperately needed to relieve herself after a long night at sea. But she wished to keep the truth unheard. So her eyes dropped to the creaky wooden floor where they planned to stay.

Captain Scarlett touched the tip of the blade to her cheek. Feeling the pressure, Elaine shut her eyes and mentally took herself out of the room, imagining that she were somewhere with Henry. As a soft circle formed between her lips, she inhaled and then blew the air out slowly.

Admiring her resting face, Captain Scarlett trailed his fingertips down the length of her cheek and along her jawline. Elaine shuddered at his touch and kept her eyes closed.

Captain Scarlett tilted his head to the side and let his hand descend to the skin along her clavicle. Following the path of desire, Captain Scarlett grasped her arms and laid her down on the cot. Then he took the blade and traced it down the length of her sternum.

Elaine lay still and forced herself to remain calm. With the slightest flutter of her long black lashes, she drew him in like a moth to a flame. He left the knife on her stomach and planted his hands along either side of her body, gazing over her beautiful face.

.

The angel on his shoulder told him to leave her alone. She was another man's wife.

But then Elaine parted her lips and tilted her head into his pillow. Unable to resist her charms, Captain Scarlett curled his hand around her back and pulled her body into him. His lips slanted over her mouth as the green apple dropped from his hand and rolled across the floor. Pulsing with passion, Captain Scarlett grabbed at her flesh and nearly groaned when he heard her sigh. He wanted to believe that no one had brought color to her cheeks before him.

Buzzing with sensation, Captain Scarlett molded his mouth to hers and threaded his fingers through her hair. Regardless of his place, he wanted to make love to her right then and there. Not because she was forbidden fruit, or even for his own pleasure. But for hers.

Elaine dug her nails into the back of his neck and turned her head to the side when his lips forged a path down her throat. As he braided his fingers through hers, Elaine sat up on the cot and freed her hands from his so she could claim his face. Then she cupped his cheeks in either of her palms and kissed him until he could scarcely breathe.

Taking control, Elaine pressed his back into the cot and rose above him, the ends of her hair touching his face. Captain Scarlett clutched her hip with a smile and treasured every kiss. As she tugged at his lower lip, Elaine held his hands above his head and gripped the knife in her hand. Alarm shot through Captain Scarlett when the cool metal blade touched his throat.

Elaine glowered down at him and pressed the sharp edge deeper into his skin.

"Captain Pierce was right," he struggled to say. "You are a clever girl."

Gritting her teeth, Elaine dug her knee into his stomach and he gasped. "If you don't hold up your end of the bargain, if you don't take me and my husband home as you have promised, I swear to God I will slit your throat in the night while you sleep."

"Is that so?" he countered. "And what will you do when I take you in the night?"

Elaine reared back and slapped him. "I am not a vessel for your pleasure."

Wincing, Captain Scarlett turned his head and spit, blood trickling down his lip.

"Promise me that you will keep your word," she demanded. "Say it!"

Captain Scarlett relaxed beneath her and smirked. "I promise to return you and your husband to America after you have held up your end of the bargain, and only then."

Staring into his brown eyes, Elaine wondered if she should include Louisa and Frederic in the agreement. But she thought his ignorance of two other allies on the island might serve as leverage later. So she bit her tongue and failed to mention them.

"Anything else you would like to add, Mrs. Rochester?" Captain Scarlett should have kicked himself for the slip up, but there was no disguising what he knew.

Enraged by his deception, Elaine hit him in the jaw and then tossed him onto the hard ground. As wooden boards pounded against his back, Captain Scarlett rolled over and twisted his arms together. Elaine leapt down from the cot and ran for the door. But when she reached the other side of the captain's quarters, the door was locked.

"No!" Elaine cried, kicking her bare foot against the wood. Her eyes stung with tears from the pain it caused, as she pressed her forehead to the door. "No," she breathed.

Taking pity on her, Captain Scarlett got to his feet and trudged all the way over to her. "What did you expect? That I would leave the door unlocked for you to run off in the night?"

When Elaine turned back to him, Captain Scarlett placed his hands on either side of the door and caged her in with his arms. She nearly burst into tears at the realization that her act had been all for nothing. But then he knelt down and lifted the hem of her gown.

"No. Don't!" she begged, peering down at him with fear in her eyes.

Rolling his eyes, Captain Scarlett took the knife from her hand and slipped it into the sheath along her thigh. Elaine breathed a sigh of relief as he lowered her gown to cover the rest of her legs and rose to his feet. "For a moment there, I almost believed you loved me."

Something caught in the back of Elaine's throat. Remorse? Guilt? Empathy?

She had played him for a fool, but he was the one holding her captive.

"Dry your eyes," he commanded. "The men will think I have done something to you."

Elaine dragged the back of her hand across the mess of tears and failed to understand the trembling sensation in the pit of her stomach. "I think I'm going to be sick."

Captain Scarlett reached around her waist to unlock the door and motioned for her to step outside. Searching for a bucket, Elaine ran up the staircase and found one above deck for her to vomit in. Once she finished, Elaine sat down on her knees and pressed her forehead against a wooden post. Her body was damp with sweat, but she felt cool.

Crouching down beside her, Captain Scarlett touched her shoulder and smoothed his fingers through her long black hair. "Are you all right? Today, we must hunt. I can't have you wandering about in the jungle with a bucket ready to be sick."

With her eyes closed, Elaine drew in a deep breath. "The sickness has passed."

"Very well." Captain Scarlett rose to his feet as the morning sun beat upon his back. "I am desperate to find five big cats in the jungle. At least two to start with today."

"I don't know if I can lead you to them that quickly," she began, clutching her mouth. "Especially since you have just arrived with your ship and crew. They will have heard the noise and retreated deeper into the jungle. Animals are not foolish, you know."

"Yes, I know," Frederic replied. "Mother Nature has left all of that up to us."

Chapter 13

Elaine pressed the flat of her palm against her stomach as Captain Scarlett led her off the ship. As numbers ran circles in her mind, she ticked one date off after the other, relying on approximation since there were no calendars on the island. It was then that it occurred to her what must have been the cause for her sudden morning sickness. She was pregnant.

As reality dawned on her, Elaine treaded across the sand with a wave of panic sprouting from the very pit of her soul. How could this have happened again? That Elaine had conceived a child while on the island, and she couldn't even find Henry and tell him? Because she had no earthly idea where he was.

"You cannot take this many men." Elaine turned around at the sight of an army approaching. Thoughts of the baby huddled at the back of her mind for now.

"And why on earth not?" Captain Scarlett

angled the black hat on his head, that ridiculous ruby colored plume whipping in the wind.

"Because it will cause too much noise, and you will scare them off," she explained.

"Well, how many am I to bring then?" Captain Scarlett stayed by her side and scanned her face. Just twelve hours and he was already infatuated with her. What was it about this island girl? What made her so different?

Elaine searched the party of men before her, spotting an elderly gentleman with thin white hair. He wore a pair of skinny wire-rimmed glasses, and his hands were in chains.

"Five," Elaine answered, tearing her eyes away from the old man.

"In addition to us?" Captain Scarlett gestured between the two of them.

"No." Elaine briefly shut her eyes in frustration. "Including us."

Rolling his eyes, Captain Scarlett stuck his thumb and middle finger between his lips and whistled. "All right, lads! Everyone but you three head back to the ship. Captain's orders."

Elaine looked out at the candidates he had chosen and wasn't the least bit excited to find that Connell was among them. He licked his lips and strode past Elaine, brushing her arm in the process. Then a plump beefy man with streaky dark hair and a beard with flecks of orange in it dragged the old man in chains behind him.

Something tugged at Elaine's heartstrings as the

old man walked past her and smiled. Why did he look so familiar? Had she known him in New York? Had he been a business associate of Philip's? Even though she believed that she had never been formally introduced, there was something about the man that turned her head to the side.

"Connell?" Captain Scarlett wagged a finger at the cocky young man until he sauntered back over. "If you would," he suggested, nodding his head in Elaine's direction.

With a teasing smirk, Connell grabbed Elaine's wrists and sought to bind them with rope.

"What are you doing?" Elaine struggled, elbowing Connell in the ribs when he proved resilient. He wrapped his arm around her stomach and pulled her back into his chest, leaning his chin over her shoulder to secure the rope around her wrists.

"How am I to lead you into the jungle without worrying that you might run off?" Captain Scarlett held her glistening green glower and then flicked his eyes to Connell.

The rope burned her wrists as she seethed with fury. Once he was finished, Connell smoothed his finger along her cheek and tugged her chin up. Recoiling at his touch, Elaine jerked away and spit in his face.

When Connell lunged forward to slap her, Captain Scarlett intervened and grabbed the man by the collar of his shirt. "Do not touch her ever again," he growled, pushing Connell with enough force for him to fall flat on his face.

Gritting his teeth, Connell stood up and brushed the sand from his clothing. When he stalked off to follow the other two into the jungle, Captain Scarlett felt glorious for staking his claim on the girl. Elaine looked over at him in surprise and muttered, "Thank you."

At the sight of her smile, Captain Scarlett's lip twitched and curved upward in delight. Unable to resist, he took a step towards her and brushed the back of his knuckles against her cheek. "I won't let him harm you, Ms. Carmichael. I promise."

She nodded at the kind gesture. Captain Scarlett had staked his claim on Elaine, but that might not bode well for her by the time the month was up.

"Shall we?" Captain Scarlett extended his hand towards the jungle.

Without a word, Elaine stepped forward and followed the footprints in the sand that the men before her had made. Captain Scarlett remained at her side with his dagger drawn.

Pulling in a quick breath, Elaine glided across the sand and into the forest, lifting her eyes to the tree tops above. She hoped that Louisa had hidden herself away and found either Henry or Frederic to guard her in the night. With Judas still lurking and Captain Scarlett onshore with nearly thirty men, the odds were hardly in her favor.

For the first time, Elaine spotted the rifle in

Connell's hands. She tightened her throat and swallowed at the significance of the weapon in his grip. He led the line ahead of the old man and his guard, while Captain Scarlett rested his hand along the small of her back.

Sunshine flickered through the trees as the group advanced deeper into the forest. After nearly half an hour of creeping through the thickets, Captain Scarlett took Elaine's elbow and steered her towards the front of the group. She shuddered at the glower on Connell's face when they passed him by, and Captain Scarlett distanced them from the rest.

"Now, Ms. Carmichael." Captain Scarlett parked her before a great tree and looked down, his brown eyes flitting across her alluring features. "Lead me to your creatures."

With the utmost regret, she kept her head down and nodded. Forgive me Jade, she thought, chanting the words over and over in her head like a mantra.

Even though she had been taken and commanded by force, Elaine could not escape the surmounting guilt swelling within her chest. Animals of the wild were meant to be left alone, only attacked as the result of self-defense, or life or death, or predator versus prey.

But this was no hallmark of survival. This was an exploitation of the dear creatures by ruthless men who were controlled by power and greed. For a moment, Elaine wished she had never left the jungle. Somehow, the animals were more human than man himself.

Relying on instinct alone, Elaine knelt down behind the underbrush as Captain Scarlett crouched low alongside her. He waved his arm and gestured for the remaining men to join him and fan out to his left, nowhere near Elaine. He turned his head to watch her, but her gaze was readily fixed somewhere else.

Elaine looked out at the clear running brook up ahead. Just a couple days ago, Henry had laid her body down in the grass and touched Elaine in ways that made her unravel. Her cheeks flushed at the recent memory and a glistening teardrop skirted down her face. For the memory of his body all around her had become the most distant of all.

Waiting patiently, Captain Scarlett watched the rushing water and wondered at her intuition. For months, he had imagined the island girl Captain Pierce had spoken of, with features so enchanting that it was impossible for them to be real. Despite the vivid fantasy, Elaine was so much more than he could have imagined. Even more alluring in person.

"Captain," Connell grunted at an approaching animal.

Elaine knelt down and bit her lip, her chest rising and falling with pain. A long lithe leopard strode towards the brook and lowered its head to the cool water. Calm and reserved, the creature flicked its tongue out and then looked up at nothing in particular.

"All right," Captain Scarlett hissed at Connell. "Now."

"NO!" Elaine screamed the second Connell fired the rifle.

The leopard flicked its ears at the sound and tensed to run away. But the bullet pierced its heart before it could flee the area. Connell fired another shot to be sure, and the big cat staggered forward, losing balance and the ability to keep its weight on all four paws.

As tears streamed down her cheeks, Elaine darted from the brush and waded through the brook until she reached the leopard's side. Panting aloud, the jungle cat set its head on the ground and widened its blue eyes up at Elaine. Even with her hands tied, Elaine reached out and planted her palm along the leopard's gold belly, spotted with eye-catching rosettes. The beautiful black markings were not meant for some shiny new coat.

"I'm sorry," Elaine cried, holding eye contact with the creature. "Forgive me."

Fighting for air, the leopard drew in a final breath and then every bit of light left its eyes.

"No!" Elaine moaned. "No, no, no..." Her hands were covered in blood as she crumpled deeper into the ground and mourned for the loss of the leopard.

Captain Scarlett, Connell, and the others stood on the opposite side of the brook in fascination and awe. How could the girl have so much feeling for an animal? It was merely a beast, and would have surely killed her when it was time to eat. Where was the harm?

When Elaine caught them gawking, she rose up and crossed the channel of water. The moment her foot touched land, Elaine shouted and cursed at Connell, kicking him in the shins until he restrained her. Connell pressed his arm against her abdomen and squeezed until the flat of her back slammed into his hard chest. Throbbing with vengeance, she bucked against him and sank her teeth into the flesh of his arm.

"Ah!" Connell released Elaine and tossed her to the ground. "She bit me!"

Looking over the matter with a sigh, Captain Scarlett motioned to the guard watching the man in chains and nodded Connell in the same direction. Before they could plunge into the water, a frolicking leopard cub rolled through the underbrush and onto the river bank. Letting out a baby cough, the cub slowly approached its dead mother and reached a paw out to touch her body. Then the infant leopard nuzzled closer and cried out.

"Look what you've done," Elaine accused, still shaking with grief on the ground.

Connell and the guard proceeded into the brook and stood along either side of the leopard once they reached the other side. Frightened by strangers, the leopard cub reared back and ran off into the wilderness, tearing through the trees. Elaine's lower lip trembled at the sight, for there was a time when that very cub had been little Jade.

Captain Scarlett knelt down to help Elaine to her feet. But she rebelled against the captain and elbowed him in the jaw when he tried to pull her upright. Wincing in pain, Captain Scarlett refrained from touching her and rubbed his jaw.

"I hate you," she cried, tearing her palms across her eyes. "I hate you!"

When Elaine leaned over and struck him, Captain Scarlett was astounded at the damage she could do with a pair of bound wrists. He braced her shoulders and held her still until she stopped fighting him, stroking her back in reassurance. She buried her face in her hands and cried as he wrapped his arms around her body and held her close.

"Might I remind you that you agreed to this, Ms. Carmichael," he said, combing his fingers through the hair over her shoulders. "It is part of our deal."

Elaine looked into his dark eyes and whispered, "To you, she may have just been a shortcut to a fortune." She turned her line of sight to the dead leopard on the ground. "But she was much more than that," Elaine sobbed. "You killed a mother."

Captain Scarlett furrowed his brow and gazed upon her face with wonder. As Connell and the guard tugged at the body of the leopard and then lifted it, the captain felt a pang of remorse shudder through his chest over the cries of the cub. Elaine rocked back and got to her feet without help from any man. His eyes followed her as she walked away, taking a seat at the edge of the brook to stare blankly ahead at the tapestry of liquid glass.

Chapter 14

Snapping his head up at the sound of a gunshot, Henry Rochester flicked his eyes to the skyline and wondered. Frederic roused awake with Louisa in his arms, while she rubbed the sleep from her eyes. "What was that?" Frederic mused, immediately alert.

Henry held a finger to his lips and marched off in the direction of the noise.

"Henry. Wait." Louisa stood up and brushed the dirt from her dress, while Frederic took her hand and followed in Henry's footsteps.

"Perhaps we should have ambushed the ship last night," Henry remarked. "What if we are late?" He shot an apprehensive look their way. "What if we have waited too long?"

At the sound of another gunshot, Louisa's sparkling blue eyes widened in terror. While they had no way of knowing how many men were aboard the ship, Frederic had given a fairly accurate approximation. About thirty seamen between captain and crew.

Henry's golden eyes drifted through the trees as he perked his ears up to listen.

"Surely, the whole lot of them would not go trekking through the forest," Frederic gathered. His arm remained around Louisa's waist as Henry crept deeper into the wilderness. "We would have heard a party that large walking by. I know we would've."

With a hand gesture that indicated Frederic should remain quiet, Henry took one careful footstep in front of the other and motioned for Frederic and Louisa to follow. All three of them scanned the forest as they plunged deeper into the jungle.

By the time Henry heard voices, Frederic and Louisa crouched down behind the cover of ever-tangling undergrowth among the thickets. Henry ducked down alongside them and squatted low enough to not be discovered. As he peered through the trees, a head covered in long, lustrous black hair came into view. It belonged to the body of a beautiful woman with honey golden skin and glistening green eyes.

At the first recognition of Elaine, Henry's heart nearly skipped a beat. She was alive.

But then a large hand settled on her back, a rough dirty hand that belonged to another man. Jealousy and anger shot through Henry, nearly compelling him to run after her and tackle the man to the ground. But that would have revealed their hiding place, which was the only advantage they had at present.

As the other members of the party came into view, Frederic rose up and gasped, "Father."

Louisa grabbed his arm and jerked him back down alongside her. "Have you gone mad?"

Frederic swallowed and remembered his place in the jungle among pirates. Then he flitted his gray eyes back up to the old man in chains, lingering several footsteps behind Elaine. There was a reason why he had recognized the white sails of Captain Scarlett's ship. Because it was the one who had taken his father and was holding him captive at present.

"Which man, Frederic?" Louisa whispered. "Which man is responsible?"

Frederic gazed out with a keen eye and spotted him. "That one." He pointed his finger at a tall man with dark hair and olive skin, the same who pressed his hand into the small of Elaine's back. "You see his hat?" Frederic motioned to the black hat with that red plume feather peeking out of the top of it. "Yes, that is him. I'm sure of it."

Henry narrowed his eyes with anger. "What is his name?"

"Captain Scarlett," another voice answered. Judas materialized behind them, encircled Louisa with one arm and placed a knife to her throat. "Be very quiet."

Henry and Frederic reached for their weapons, but Judas had already pulled Louisa back and clamped his other hand down over her mouth. She whimpered in shock, breathing through her nose the best she could. The blade felt awfully cold and sharp against the pulsing point in her neck. One wrong move and the blood would be gushing.

"Do not make a sound as they pass by," he demanded. "If you call out to them for help, I will slit her throat." He pressed the blade in deeper and the hair stood up on the back of her neck.

Gritting his teeth, Frederic turned to look at Henry and exhaled hot air through his nostrils. Both men stayed hidden in the underbrush and watched their only chance for help drift off into the distance. Perhaps it was a long shot anyway. Because what were the odds that Captain Scarlett would not be on Judas's side anyway?

Once the last man disappeared into the forest, Henry turned back and pulled out his dagger. Frederic did the same as they approached Judas. But he merely took another step back with Louisa and two for every step they took forward.

"What do you want?" Frederic snapped, seething with fury at Judas.

"I'm surprised to find you so wholly altered, Freddy." Judas trailed his nose along the side of Louisa's neck. "Has she instilled this change in you? Perhaps I should have a taste."

"No!" Frederic lunged forward and Judas pushed the edge of the blade against her skin.

Henry gripped his dagger and then ripped his

fingers through his dark locks. Why was it that Judas always knew exactly how to leverage the situation? Had there even been an occasion when he did not possess the upper hand?

"What do you want?" Henry asked. "Whatever it is, we will help you find it."

"What?" Frederic intervened, casting his eyes on Henry. "No."

"What do you think of this, dear Louisa?" Judas breathed down her neck. "Internal discord. A rift between brother and beau. Whose side will you choose?"

Henry tensed his jaw and cornered Judas with a piercing gleam. Although it was merely a delusion, for Judas could never be cornered. It was the most infuriating truth about him.

"Just tell us what you want, Judas," Henry announced, grabbing his attention.

Judas grinned at Henry and then turned his attention to Frederic. "Treasure."

"Treasure?" Henry echoed. "What are you talking about? You took all of it!"

Blinking in disbelief, Judas lowered his chin and only glimpsed Henry for a moment.

"You broke into my father's safe and burned down the factory to cover your tracks," Henry reported. "How can you demand treasure when you know that you have already taken it?"

"Frederic has seen the treasure," Judas replied. "Have you not?"

When Frederic bowed his head, Henry scoffed

in outrage.

"As well as sweet Louisa here." Judas grabbed her chin and she squirmed.

"Frederic, what is he talking about?" Henry stepped towards him with a dark furrowed brow.

"Yes, Frederic!" Judas mimicked. "What am I talking about?"

Henry flitted his eyes between both men, wishing that Elaine were here. She had better intuition than him and relied on her instincts wholeheartedly. Honestly, he felt like a coward and a fool. He should have chased after that man with the red feather in his hat and rescued Elaine from him. Why were he and Frederic so helpless at protecting the women they held most dear? The captains always seemed to be three steps ahead.

"All I am asking is that you show me where it is," Judas finally said. "And darling Louisa here will go free." He smelled her blonde hair and a shiver traveled down her spine.

"How can we trust you?" Henry asked. "How do I know you will stay true to your word?"

Henry's skin prickled with fear when Judas laughed. "How can you trust me? What I want to know is how you can trust Frederic. My right hand man of all people."

Henry pinned his eyebrows together and regarded Frederic with doubt. While he had taken his time in warming up to the kidnapper and thief, Henry wondered why he had ever accepted him at all. Judas was transparent now that they were in the jungle, no longer passing himself off as the honorable Captain William Pierce. But what of Frederic?

"He kidnapped your sister and brought her here because I told him to!" Judas squeezed his arm around Louisa's waist and pointed the tip of the knife at Frederic.

Henry lowered the dagger to his side and mulled over the matter.

"How can you trust his word, Henry?" Judas stared into his golden brown eyes, easily swayed and duped without that pretty wife by his side. "Frederic Holmes is a street rat! A liar and a thief! Why do you think I brought him here? Why do you think he is working for me?"

"Henry," Frederic sighed, fighting to pull the questioning man's gaze in his direction. "The old man you saw back there in chains? He is my father. I am to do as Judas says for a year before he will let my father go free. That is the only reason I ever took Louisa!"

"He's lying," Judas intervened, setting his cobalt eyes on Henry.

Dropping his eyes to the ground, Henry recalled Elaine sharing the reasons behind Frederic's criminal ways. While she had undoubtedly been told the same story by Frederic, surely Elaine could sense the truth teller from the liar. So Henry chose to believe Frederic.

"Have you truly found the treasure?" Henry gazed up at Frederic.

"Yes," he answered, a sudden breeze drifting through his auburn hair.

"All right then, Judas." Henry clasped his palms together. "We will take you to it."

"Don't trust him, Henry!" Frederic grabbed Henry's arm. "He'll go back on his word. I've seen it," he confessed, shaking Henry's shoulders. "Don't play his game."

Henry took Frederic off to the side and kept his voice down. "While I agree with you, I don't see any other way about the matter. He has Louisa, Frederic. What more can we do?"

Louisa held her breath as Frederic and Henry talked. She shut her eyes as Judas ran his fingers along her neck, hardly able to believe that his affection was something she had once longed for. How foolish—so much like a child—she had been.

"All right, Judas." Henry placed his hands on his belt and walked over to the man holding his sister. "Frederic will take you to the treasure, so long as you let Louisa go."

Judas blinked several times, weighing his stance in the matter. "We will all stay together then," he suggested. "Here in the jungle. All four of us."

Henry furrowed his brow at the odd suggestion. "Yes. I suppose so."

With a suggestive smirk, Judas released Louisa and she ran into Frederic's arms. Though he would never say it, an unfamiliar emotion pierced through Judas's heart at the sight of his former fiancé so intimately wrapped up in the warm embrace of another man. Perhaps he was jealous. Perhaps he was angry. Perhaps he was hurt.

Chapter 15

By nightfall, Elaine lay on the cot in the captain's cabin. With her face turned to the wall, she clutched her stomach and longed for Henry. The pain of watching the leopard get killed today and the poor baby cub who had to cry and suffer as a result made her think of Lilly home alone in New York. Did she miss her mother? Did she miss her father? Did she even know who they were?

When the door creaked open, Captain Scarlett slipped into the room and swiftly shut the door behind him. He moistened his lower lip and stepped across the wooden boarding of the floor, removing his hat and placing it on the desk. At the sight of Elaine weeping in his cot, pain tugged at his heart, lancing right through it like a knife.

Captain Scarlett sighed and moved towards her. He longed to reach out and touch her warm body, comfort her. But he knew that she must hate him.

"Ms. Carmichael," he crooned above her. "Are you all right?"

Elaine fluttered her lashes and pressed the tip of her finger against the wall.

Captain Scarlett sat down on the edge of the cot and rested his elbows along his knees. With a dulling sigh, he felt the heat of her body close and desired to draw near.

"You're a murderer," Elaine whispered. She curled into a ball on the cot and stared straight ahead. Tears streamed down her eyes, though she made no intention of wiping them away.

While he should have taken offense, Captain Scarlett merely folded his fingers together and exhaled. "I find value in nature and share its beauty with the world."

Elaine scowled at that attempt of a response. Shaking her head, she leaned back on her elbows and glared at him with water in her eyes. "You find beautiful creatures and exploit them. You steal life from them. You steal motherhood from them. You kill them."

Captain Scarlett tilted his chin and narrowed his eyes at her strange opinion. "From what I recall, Ms. Carmichael, you agreed to help me search in the jungle. You know what I am. You know my intentions for them. So why did you help me do it?"

Elaine clenched her jaw and snarled, "Because you made me."

When Elaine put her head back down,

Captain Scarlett admired her lustrous black hair in the moonlight. How he longed to run his fingers through those smooth dark locks. But that luxury belonged to another man. Her husband, the man whose last name she bore. Henry.

"I never meant to upset you," Captain Scarlett murmured. He grimaced immediately, hardly able to believe that he had uttered those words. What had she done to him?

"Well, you have," was her only reply.

As Elaine breathed in and out, Captain Scarlett watched the rise and fall of her back. Surely, the month would pass by quicker than he wished. And then she would be gone. Forever.

"It was you," Elaine gasped in realization. She pressed her palms into the mattress and sat up, glancing back at him in horror. "Wasn't it?"

"Whatever are you speaking of now?" Captain Scarlett asked with a stare.

Swallowing to force the lump down her throat, Elaine placed her hand at the base of her neck and shuddered. "Jade," she whispered. "You cut out her eyes, stuffed her head."

Captain Scarlett looked away and hung his head, for it was undoubtedly true.

Elaine sniffled and dabbed at her tears with a sob. "She was my friend."

"She was a creature!" Captain Scarlett barked. "An animal. Why, I bet she would even eat you if she were hungry enough." He paused for a beat. "She was a beast."

Clenching her jaw with hatred, Elaine reached out and slapped him. Captain Scarlett shut his eyes at the harsh sting and pressed his lips together as well. Somehow, he found pleasure in the pain, because it might be the only way she ever touched him voluntarily.

"I want Henry," Elaine cried, blinking back her tears. "I want my husband."

"Well, you're not going to get him!" Captain Scarlett snapped back.

Her eyes dilated in panic as the captain looked over at her and rose to his feet. Deep down, he would give anything for Elaine to cry out for him, to crave his touch, to say his name. But it was never going to happen, and that only made him want her more.

"But you promised." Her lower lip trembled as the wind drifted from her sails.

A pitiful look fell over the face of the captain. One that he would rather not have expressed. His hands lingered by his sides, and when he balled them into fists, blue veins raised in patterns across the back of them. Tension radiated throughout his body—the kind that he just couldn't handle at the moment.

"Yes, I promised you, dearie. But didn't anyone ever tell you not to strike a bargain with the devil?" He tore his eyes away from hers and strode towards the door.

"You're not like him." Her soft voice carried across the room and stopped the captain in his tracks.

Turning back to her, he lifted his chin and asked, "Not like whom?"

"Judas," Elaine answered. "Or Captain William Pierce, as you know him."

Captain Scarlett crossed his arms over his chest and took a few steps towards her. She utterly defied him, drawing the captain back in when he was moments away from fleeing the room. He was the moth. And she was the flame.

"I know you're different," she demanded, wringing her hands with passion. "You have never treated me the way he does. If you only knew the wicked things he would like to do to me."

Captain Scarlett took another step forward and balled his hand into a fist at her words.

"He is not honorable." Elaine toyed with the thin white sheet over the cot and gazed out the window. "What is your name, Captain Scarlett? Your real name?"

Surprised by her question, Captain Scarlett moved close enough to reach his desk and leaned against the edge. "Gregory," he confessed, for there was no harm in telling her.

"May I call you Gregory?" She sounded sweet as she stared into his eyes.

"Yes, Mrs. Rochester." He set the heel of his palm against the desk. "You may."

"Have you ever been in love?"

It was an odd question, especially coming from the woman who had just slapped him. But Captain

Scarlett found himself enjoying her sudden curiosity. Perhaps she cared about his heart. The irony was, she would be the only one to ever break it.

"No." Captain Scarlett narrowed his eyes. "I have not had that misfortune."

Turning her head, Elaine stared through the glass at moonlight pouring over the sea. "Well, that is a shame. I pity you Gregory, even if it is only for that."

Captain Scarlett chuckled. "I can assure you that I do not require your pity."

"Is that so?" Elaine leaned her chin back until her head pressed against the wall. Her eyes lingered on the jostling waves before connecting with his across the room.

"Yes," he hissed. His heart was pounding as blood thrummed loudly in his ears. He wanted to scream in her face and kiss her all at the same time. What was it about this island girl? Even Judas had fallen prey to her charms. What made her so different?

"Then I will tell you about my love," she revealed, "since you know nothing of it."

At first, Captain Scarlett was struck with the urge to hold up his hand in an attempt to silence her. But as the words rolled off her tongue, he found himself genuinely interested in whatever she had to say. So he remained as he was and let her talk.

"I was stranded on this island for years," she

began. "And then one day, Henry washed ashore, shipwrecked just the same as I. Jade attacked him, because she wanted to protect me. So I tended to his wounds and taught him how to live off the land."

Captain Scarlett tilted his head and stroked the whiskers along his chin with a sigh, feigning boredom and disinterest. In all honesty, he longed to hear every word out of her mouth. He didn't want her to stop.

"We fell in love." Elaine searched her palms, braiding her fingers together as she reminisced about that time. "And he is a good man. We have a daughter."

The mere mention of a child tugged at his heartstrings, especially a child of hers. And a daughter. She must have looked just like her. Elaine in the earliest stage of youth.

"You must be able to understand how difficult it is for me to be away from her." Elaine lifted her eyes to meet Captain Scarlett's resilient gaze. He was so focused on her every word that it nearly made her tremble. "So the separation from my husband makes the situation all the more painful. But I will be reunited with them both. I must."

Captain Scarlett dragged his teeth over his lower lip and pushed off the edge of the desk. He strode towards the window with his arms at his sides and looked out at the water. "I never would have imagined that you had a daughter, Ms. Carmichael."

Elaine watched him from the cot in the hope that he might develop some empathy at the reality of her words. Surely, any decent man could have compassion for a mother and her child. "Well I do, Gregory. And I miss her very much. Not a day goes by that I don't think of her. And I am sure that I can say the same for Henry as well."

Still looking through the glass, Captain Scarlett dropped his gaze to the bottom end of the window. "What is her name?" he wondered. "Your daughter, I mean."

Surprised that he cared to know, Elaine smiled at the thought of her and replied, "Lilly. After my mother, Lillian. She passed away many years ago, but I think of her often."

Nodding at her admission, Gregory turned back to her no matter the swelling pride in his chest. Perhaps it was finally time to confess the truth to someone. To let out what had been resting on his heart. To expose the burden on his back that he had carried for years.

"I had a daughter once," he began. "She died along with her mother at childbirth."

"Gregory, I'm so sorry." Elaine furrowed her brow in sympathy. "I didn't know."

"Well, I suppose it doesn't matter anymore." He turned his eyes back on the glass, a point of return where he could look when the feelings became too much. "She is gone."

Capitalizing on his state of vulnerability, Elaine stared at the back of his head and sighed. She might as well ask the question, because there was no better time than now.

"Will you let me see my husband? Will you take us home to our daughter?"

"Yes," Captain Scarlett agreed. "But I require something of you in return."

Gazing at him in innocence, Elaine clung to the bed sheet when he slowly stalked towards her. Captain Scarlett came close enough to touch, though he did not touch her. Her breath caught at the back of her throat as she widened her eyes in surprise.

"You must help me find another cat." He held a finger in the air and stared down at her with longing. "One more, Ms. Carmichael. That is all that I ask."

Captain Scarlett turned on his heel and left her to sleep alone in his cabin. Once he shut the door behind him, he sank down to the floor and reached for a bottle of rum. For the life of him, he could not understand why he kept calling her Ms. Carmichael, when she was indeed Mrs. Rochester.

He took a long pull on the bottle and leaned his head back. Swiping his fingertips along his brow, Captain Scarlett sighed as the stunning truth sank in. Ms. Carmichael implied that she was unmarried, unattached, and maybe even yet to receive the affection of a man. But Mrs. Rochester—that implied the opposite of all three. She would never belong to him.

Chapter 16

At the break of dawn, Frederic roused awake with Louisa in his arms. Along with Henry, the two men had taken shifts watching Judas in the night. With him so close, neither trusted that he would not bring harm to Louisa while they slept.

Henry stood at a nearby tree with his hand clutching the dagger at his belt. Judas was sitting on a boulder with his ankle across his thigh, his cobalt eyes readily fixed on Louisa. She had slept with her palm placed over Frederic's heart, and Judas could not stand it.

Sheer jealousy ate Judas up inside, because he had never intended Louisa to be more than a pawn. She was young and foolish, easy prey for a predator of Judas's type. One without cause or conscience. But now that she had leapt into the arms of another man so easily, Judas could not help loathing her.

Louisa should have been love struck over Judas, her every emotion paralyzed the moment she discovered his true nature. So how had she been able to move on so quickly? Did Frederic Holmes really have that much more to offer her?

Judas had an island. Frederic had an elderly father in chains.

With a breathy sigh, Louisa yawned and snuggled into Frederic's body. Judas picked up a flat stone to sharpen the blade of his knife and boiled red hot with anger.

"You've slept long enough!" Judas abruptly stood and tossed the stone to the ground. Rearing back, Louisa cuddled deeper into Frederic which only made Judas hate him more.

"Leave her alone," Frederic defended. "She has just woken up."

Judas scoffed and stormed off, while Henry looked to his sister and Frederic with the shake of his head. Pushing the matter aside, Frederic got to his feet and helped Louisa to do the same. When she stood up and leaned into his body, Frederic took her hand and led her towards Henry. All three kept quiet and followed the way Judas had gone.

After ten minutes of trudging, Frederic proclaimed, "You are going the wrong way."

Judas froze in his tracks with a sneer on his face. "Really? Then which is the right way, Mr. Holmes? Would you like to lead us to the treasure?"

Surprised by his disgruntled tone, Henry grabbed Judas's arm and asked, "What is the matter? He will take you to the treasure. Isn't that the only thing you came here for?"

Judas gritted his teeth and practically growled at Henry. Then his frightening blue eyes shifted to Louisa. Frederic caught on and pushed her body behind his own for protection.

"Yes," Judas scowled. "I suppose it is."

"Go on ahead, Frederic," Henry directed, pointing in that direction with his finger. "God knows I haven't a clue where it is."

Nodding in agreement, Frederic wrapped his arm around Louisa and led her away. She looked back over his shoulder at Judas and stared. Then Frederic regained her attention, and Louisa clung to his side as they walked on ahead of the group.

"What do you plan to do with it?" Henry inquired, treading the ground beside him.

"With what?" Judas fired back, angry and defensive.

Henry looked straight ahead, his eyes on Frederic and Louisa. "Why, the treasure, of course!" he chuckled, and the sullen sound did not sit well with Judas.

"I haven't thought of it." Judas stared at the back of Louisa's head.

"You will have access to all in the world that money can buy," Henry noted. "I wonder..." He stopped and Judas halted as well. "What will your first purchase be?"

Judas regarded Henry for a moment, wondering if in another life they might have been friends. Surely, a false reality where he could marry Louisa and have Henry for a brother-in-law. Why hadn't that been his destiny? Why couldn't he have been born a poor gentleman rather than a wealthy scoundrel?

"What I most desire cannot be bought." Realizing his mistake in discretion, Judas hurried onward in the hope that Henry had not caught on to his meaning.

"Something priceless?" Henry probed. "I wonder what that could be?"

"Don't stand there and act as though you understand my situation in life." Judas stalked closer and glowered at Henry with hatred. "Rich boy born to a rich father who lives in a rich house. That is your story Henry, and your destiny as well."

"And what is yours?" Henry fired back, discovering his weakest points.

"My father picked pockets for a living, and my mother was a whore."

Henry blinked and crossed his arms over his chest. "And now you murder and rape."

Thriving with bloodlust, Judas forced a sinister smile. "Oh yes. It is my destiny."

Henry shook his head in disapproval and took a step forward to catch up with Frederic and Louisa. It had been a bad idea to talk some sense into the man in the hope of retribution. Judas had relinquished Louisa, and Henry had an inkling that Judas might be able to help them take Elaine out from under Captain Scarlett's nose as well.

"Perhaps you chose this life," Henry muttered at the last.

"No." Judas narrowed his eyes at the ridiculous thought. "It chose me." When Henry slipped one hand in his pocket and increased the pace of his stride, Judas chased after him and said, "Not everyone gets to lie down with that pretty little wife of yours at night."

Clenching his jaw, Henry darted his brown eyes to Judas. "Don't speak of my wife."

"Would you like to know what I would do to her if she were mine?"

Henry hurried his steps to get away from Judas. But Judas kept coming after Henry, always right on his heels.

"First, I would gaze into those liquid green eyes of hers until it made her squirm."

Henry felt the anger rising up inside of him, as he tried to reach Frederic and Louisa. But they always seemed too far ahead, while Judas briskly strolled at his side.

"Then I would put my fingers in that raven black hair and breathe her in."

Henry was not a fool. He knew the intent of Judas's game. But try as he might, Henry could not shake the mental image of Judas with Elaine from his mind.

"Then I would reach my hand out to feel that soft, smooth flesh and squeeze."

Henry turned on a dime and tackled Judas to

the ground. "Now that's enough!"

Judas lay pinned beneath him, just as planned. "She would prefer me to you. If you had only let me have her. I just needed one chance, and she never would have returned for your love."

Henry grabbed his shoulders and slammed his body into the ground. In a flash, Henry was wild and fuming, holding the steely cut blade of a knife to Judas's throat.

"That's what you want. Isn't it?" Judas pushed. "To kill me?"

Plagued by mind games, Henry closed his mouth and exhaled aloud.

"A good death," Judas carried on. "It is what I deserve."

Realizing his place, Henry backed away from Judas and rose to his feet. Despite the utter evil with which he committed crimes, Henry realized that death was no good for Judas. It was too good for him in fact.

No longer allowing himself to feed into Judas's cruel mind games, Henry turned away and walked off. Frederic and Louisa stood in silence as their eyes drifted to Judas, for they had seen the whole thing. Realizing that he did not have the power to defeat Henry, Judas collected himself and rose from the ground.

After walking through the wilderness in silence, Frederic took Louisa's arm and turned at another set of trees. The hot spring sat before them as if they had never left it.

Henry approached with wonder and bemusement on his face. He had never glimpsed water so strangely colored in all his life. Emerald at the center with a ring of sapphire around it. Surely, such a sight only occurred in folklore and fairytales.

Judas furrowed his brow as he trudged over to the hot spring. In all honesty, he had left the hiding to Samson and Peter, never anticipating that Elaine and Henry would kill them. How could he have anticipated that they were inhabiting the island?

"Well," Judas snarled, impatient as ever. "Where is it?"

Louisa looked over at him with a sense of calm. With Frederic by her side, she no longer feared the man who had once been her betrothed, who she had once dreamed of marrying, who she had once imagined to be the father of her children.

"In there." Frederic tilted his head towards the colorful water.

Judas laughed in mock amusement. "You honestly expect me to believe the treasure is in there?" He knelt down and scanned the surface. "In some godawful spring?"

"It is in there," Louisa insisted. "I've seen it."

Frederic tightened his grip around her arm, fearful that Judas might use her knowledge against her. Perhaps Louisa should have kept her mouth shut. Then again, Judas was bound to find out anyway. What did it matter who was the bearer of the news?

"Fine then." Judas crossed his arms over his chest in disbelief. "Show me."

Louisa drew deeper into Frederic's warm protection and embrace.

"Go in and find the treasure. Take some of it and bring it back for me to see."

"No," Frederic protested. "It is too dangerous."

"But I've already swam in it before," Louisa answered. "I am the only one."

Silence fell over the three men, as Louisa could see that she was the one placed with the task again. Only, she didn't feel afraid. It was the black panther who had led her to the spring, and ultimately the treasure in the first place. And she trusted the creature, no matter what anyone else thought or said.

"Louisa, I do not believe it is wise for you to go under." Henry crept closer and gazed into her eyes with careful regard and concern. "Especially since you have already taken the risk before. I do not want you to go in that water."

"I will go," Frederic volunteered, pushing himself away from Louisa.

"What?" she scanned his figure as Frederic stripped the shirt from his back.

"Your brother is right, Louisa. I cannot risk you going down there again. What if something were to happen this time? Let me go. It is simply too dangerous," Frederic agreed.

Judas rocked back on his heels and smiled. For a moment, he entertained the wicked thought of something terrible happening to Frederic while he was down there. What would darling Louisa do then? There would be no man to claim her heart. No more competition.

"Yes, Louisa." Judas grinned at her with malice. "Listen to Frederic. Let him go."

As her cheeks flushed with heat, Louisa held her chin high and glowered in Judas's direction. With the flick of his gaze, Judas dared Fredric to continue, a test of male bravado. So Frederic removed his trousers until there was nothing left but underclothing for him to plunge beneath the warm depths.

Louisa shut her eyes and held her breath, leaning into Henry's arm. Truly, she wanted to have as many steps between her and Judas as possible. Especially since he seemed to be taking so much delight in Frederic going into the spring.

Frederic inched closer and dipped his toes into the outermost ring, crinkling his nose at the retched smell of brimstone. Looking back over his shoulder, he memorized Louisa's beautiful, innocent face one last time, in case he should never get the chance to see her again. Slowly but surely, he waded into the warm water, setting his palms on the edge of the ground nearest the spring. So far, danger seemed to be the farthest thing from his path.

"How is it, Frederic?" Louisa grabbed ahold of Henry's arm and then tucked her hand through his elbow. She kept her eyes glued to Frederic and whatever might be lurking in the water.

"Warm," he noted. "As you said the other day." Growing curious, Frederic reached the centermost region and recognized the change in temperature. "It is cooler in the middle, just as you said." Frederic sifted his fingers through the emerald pool as if it were sand passing through the slits in his hand.

"Rather odd," Henry observed. "Why do you suppose that is?"

Frederic turned back and stared at the trio. "I don't know."

"Oh, I don't care!" Judas marched forward and shoved Henry and Louisa out of the way. "Just swim beneath the surface and find my treasure! Find something!"

With a resentful glower, Frederic looked over at Louisa one last time. Then he held his breath and dove beneath the still waters. Despite the slight burn, Frederic opened his eyes as he kicked his legs back and forth to propel him to the darkening depths of the spring.

As the atmosphere turned black around him, Frederic felt his heart increase in speed. A few bubbles escaped his nostrils as he hesitated for no more than a second. He could not let fear hold him back or put a hold on his mission. So he reached his arms out and swam lower and lower, trying not to worry how long he could hold his breath before he would run out of air, that is, if he even made it back to the surface.

When something glimmered in the distance, Frederic ignored the fire in his lungs and descended deeper. His body was growing weak, but he kept on until he reached a gathering of underwater boulders. Sitting there alone was one single gold coin. But everything else, the treasure Louisa had shown him before, was gone.

Confused at the disappearance, Frederic clasped the gold coin in his hand and turned to make his ascent to the surface. He could hardly stand the lack of oxygen, desperate to flail about and scream. Then an electric eel darted for him and opened his jaws.

Missing the creature by an inch, Frederic raised his arms and swam for the surface. His legs whipped back and forth like a pair of scissors as he pulled himself higher and higher, as if he were holding on to a rope and tugging while someone pulled him to the top.

When the eel followed him, Frederic closed his eyes and reached out with every breaststroke harder and faster. It seemed like an eternity had passed by the time his fingertips finally broke the surface. Rising to stand, he waded through the water and crawled to the edge of the spring, pulling himself out of there. Once he did, Frederic collapsed on the hard ground and gasped for air.

Greedy and aggressive, Judas rushed over to

Frederic and snatched the gold coin from his palm. "What is this?" Judas gripped the piece of treasure between his fingers so hard that it nearly slipped from his grasp. "You go down and return with nothing but this!"

Louisa flinched when Judas tossed the gold coin across the forest floor and it skittered up to a pair of rocks, clacking and rolling with a thud. Fearing for Frederic, Louisa knelt down beside him and touched his back as he struggled to draw enough air into his lungs. When he toppled over and lay on the flat of his back, Louisa cradled his head in her hands and stroked her fingers through his damp locks.

"A joke?" Judas accused. "Some jest! Is that what this is?"

"That is all I found, Judas," Frederic confessed. "Honestly, there is no more."

"You liar!" Judas leaned over and punched Frederic in the face.

Henry stepped between them and pushed Judas away before he could harm Frederic any more. "I think you should leave," Henry suggested. "Now. Please."

After glaring at Henry, Judas shoved him to the side and pointed a finger at Frederic. "I do not trust your word, you street rat! You have seen the treasure. I know you have. There is no point in denying it."

Frederic sat up and leaned his back into Louisa's warmth as she catered to the bloody cut across his face where Judas had struck him. He honestly had no way to prove what he saw.

"Well..." Judas waited, stomping his foot with impatience. "WHERE IS IT?"

"If you are so sure that I am not being truthful to you, then why don't you go down there and see for yourself?" Frederic challenged. "I can't imagine what could be stopping you."

Judas clenched his jaw and his cheeks smoldered. Frederic had put him in a position that would expose his cowardice should he choose to acknowledge the mission and then not accept it. It was a trick Frederic must have learned from him.

"Fine, then." Judas removed his jacket and boots, his greed surpassing a need or realization for all else. "I shall claim the treasure, rightfully so. For it was always mine."

Before they could respond, Judas stepped forward and dove into the water. When he plunged beneath the surface, Henry and Louisa moved like clockwork, leaning over the ground and taking his clothes. Bubbles rose to the surface, but they refused to let the opportunity go to waste.

With just enough time to spare, Louisa helped Frederic to his feet and the three ran, taking off into the jungle. By the time Judas surfaced with the realization that Frederic had been right—there was no treasure but the one golden coin—they were gone.

Chapter 17

C aptain Scarlett observed Elaine with careful regard as she walked out onto the deck. He took her hand with tender care and politeness, leading her to the sand along with Connell, the old man in chains, and the guard perpetually charged with the task of watching him. As her toes touched the gritty grain beneath her feet, Elaine gazed up at the wilderness ahead and wondered if she would miss the place Jade used to call home.

While she longed to be with her baby in New York, Elaine had never imagined that she would be able to return to the island. Despite the precarious circumstances, now she had finally been given the chance for a proper goodbye. Perhaps it was what she had wished for all along.

Once they reached the border of the jungle, Elaine pressed her wrists together and held them out for Connell to bind. After a restless sleep, she had decided that she would be submissive on her second and final hunt. While she loathed the killing of these beautiful creatures: Jade's cousins, brothers and sisters, Elaine knew that this was the burden she must bear to get home to her sweet baby girl. To ensure that Henry was safe. To ensure that Louisa was safe. In order to get all the things she most desired and provide protection, she would have to make the creatures a sacrifice that she would resent for the rest of her life.

"No." Captain Scarlett shook his head and lowered Elaine's hands.

"You do not wish to bind me? To keep me restrained?" She furrowed her black brow in confusion, wondering at the source of his kindness and compassion.

"No," he murmured, holding her gaze. Captain Scarlett cupped her smooth cheek in his hand. "Afterwards, you are free to go. You may be with your husband."

Wondering if she could trust his word, Elaine relaxed her shoulders with relief. Then she shed a single tear and touched the hand he had placed over her face. "Thank you."

Captain Scarlett grinned, for he had made her happy. That was all he truly wanted.

"Captain?" Connell started, pacing the border of the jungle. "Are you ready?"

Captain Scarlett acknowledged Connell for a moment and then turned his dark eyes back on Elaine. "Yes." He scanned Elaine's face and said, "We must go."

Hoping it were not too good to be true, Elaine

nodded and followed his lead. As the group plunged into the forest for a second time, Elaine lifted her eyes to the beautiful wilderness surrounding her. Would she ever get to see her home again?

Unlike yesterday, Connell led the pack with the guard and prisoner behind him. Captain Scarlett draped his arm at the small of Elaine's back, because there would soon come a time when he could never touch her again. He was not looking forward to that day.

Captain Scarlett chose a different hunting ground than yesterday, for those cats would most likely be on alert and staying well out of the way in broad daylight. Once they reached the southernmost part of the island, every man's eyes dropped down to the charred black remains of the damage the volcano had done. Elaine observed that the lava had cooled, covering all of the green and beauty of the jungle with flat black rock.

"What happened here?" Captain Scarlett took Elaine's arm and steered her towards him so she was forced to look up into his eyes.

"Volcano," she simply stated. As her vibrant green eyes raced across the land of destruction and darkness, she wondered at the animals that must have been harmed during the explosion. Just as quickly, she spotted a dead bird in the distance, with no more than a few tufts of feathers that remained. The flying creature must have put up a good fight, but in the end had not been strong enough and had lost the battle with the fiery lake of lava.

"Before I arrived?" Captain Scarlett looked over her face lovingly, hanging on her every word. When he felt her breath, it was the most wonderful feeling in the world.

"Yes," she whispered, her eyes skittering across the erosion of black.

"Well, Captain." Connell turned back with a long rifle resting in his arms. "Shall we look elsewhere?"

Captain Scarlett nodded him on, as Connell turned on his heel and led the group farther, until the jungle turned green and full of vegetation again. When they drifted beneath the shade of trees, sunlight skittering through the branches, Captain Scarlett took Elaine and brought her to the front, while the rest of the group lagged behind a pace.

"What will you do, Mrs. Rochester?" Captain Scarlett searched her eyes, desperate for them to meet his. "When you return to New York?"

Elaine stared at the ground beneath her feet. "Reunite with my family. Our little girl." She placed her hand over her stomach and smiled. "We have another little one on the way."

Captain Scarlett jerked his chin at her in surprise. "What?"

"I wish Henry was the first that I was sharing the news with," Elaine sadly remarked. Then she brought her eyes to Captain Scarlett's and sighed,

"But he is not here."

Pangs of bitter guilt and self-hatred stabbed Captain Scarlett on the inside like a knife in the chest. How could he have been so cruel? Harboring Elaine for his own malicious will? While she was carrying a child? She should have been with her husband.

Captain Scarlett took her elbow and they stopped, waving the others to go on ahead. "Why did you keep this from me?" He tilted Elaine's chin up in the palm of his hand.

"It is a matter between my husband and I," Elaine admitted. "But it is hard to keep such news to myself. Perhaps I never should have told you."

"No." Captain Scarlett shook his head and sighed. "I want to know."

At a flicker in the distance, Elaine lifted her eyes up to the highest branches of a nearby tree. The black panther with green eyes hung overhead with her tail whipping back and forth in the air. She stalked across the tree limb and stared down at the pair, but made no intention of attacking.

"Beautiful," Captain Scarlett sighed, eyeing the smooth silky nature of her fur coat.

"No!" Elaine hissed. She grabbed his arm before he could call after the others to come back. Surely, if Connell saw the jungle cat, he would raise his rifle and shoot. Elaine was going to fight with everything in her to keep that panther safe, no matter the cost.

"Ms. Carmichael." He lowered his voice and

gazed into her eyes. "It is the last one, I swear it. Can't you see? The sooner we kill this creature, the sooner you can go home. Be with your family. Be with your husband. Be with your daughter."

Elaine clenched her teeth and practically growled in his face. "Not that one."

Captain Scarlett gazed up at the gorgeous black panther and fought the urge to claim her for a new fur coat. She had perfect form, the elongated body, smooth silky black that glistened beneath flickers of sunlight. She was the most valuable specimen he had ever seen. But she was off limits. Just like her human counterpart. Mrs. Rochester.

"Not that one, Gregory," she demanded. "Not that one."

So even though it went against every desire in him, Captain Scarlett peeled his eyes away and walked off. But not without taking a final look back at the creature. She leapt from limb to limb and towered overhead, fixing those green eyes on him.

Before he could change his mind, Elaine clutched his elbow and steered him forward. "I will find you another one," she promised.

Captain Scarlett clenched his teeth and bit down, blowing hot air past his lips.

Once they caught up to the others, Elaine ordered the men to keep quiet and searched the jungle for any lurking creatures. She took careful, calculated footsteps as her green gaze remained on the treetops overhead. When her efforts proved futile, Elaine led the group back to the destruction left behind by the volcano.

"Mrs. Rochester," Captain Scarlett called. "What are you doing?"

"Shh..." she hissed, pressing a finger to her lips. "Be quiet."

He held his hands in the air and shut his mouth. After all, she knew the jungle better than him.

When Elaine motioned a hand for the rest to stay back, they watched her in curiosity and obeyed. Then she walked out and gazed at the flat black horror that covered everything that had once been beautiful and full of vegetation and life. Elaine closed her eyes and imagined what this part of the forest had once looked like.

In her vision, a black creature scuttled in her direction with a panting mouth. Then she heard the creature as well, and opened her eyes to find that it was real. A beautiful big male black panther stalked her way, though hardly had the strength to move.

Its fur had been slightly damaged from the volcano, as she saw the places on its body where lava had singed the creature. The feline pushed forward as if it were taking its last step and collapsed on the ground. Heaving for breath, the creature appeared to be in a great deal of pain. Concerned for the panther, Elaine walked towards the big cat and knelt down.

When she saw the trail of blood along its belly,

she recognized how much agony the panther had obviously been in. For days, the panther must have struggled through the jungle, surely unable to fight or fend for itself. To an enemy predator, it was dead meat.

With a tear in her eye, Elaine turned back to Connell and said, "Give me the gun."

"What's that, lass?" He looked to every man surrounding him.

Elaine rose to her feet and marched over to him, snatching the rifle from his hands when he did not offer it. He had been selfish in not handing it over sooner, for they were wasting time. The poor creature was in agony, and it could suffer for days before finally dying. She would not see the creature trapped in torment.

With a heavy heart, Elaine inhaled a shallow breath and cocked the loaded gun. Then she licked her lower lip and positioned the rifle to aim. As the creature helplessly struggled on the black burned ground, she took a deep breath and fired.

A lonesome teardrop streamed down her cheek as she watched the panther take its last breath. She was relieved that today would be her last hunt in the jungle, because she had no idea how she could ever do this again. Kill the creatures she loved most.

As the panther lay lifeless with his tongue hanging over his jaws, Elaine trudged towards the men and slammed the rifle into Connell's chest. He took a step back and gasped, the wind knocked out of him with the force she had used to give him the gun. Then Elaine bumped him in the shoulder and kept walking, hurrying her way through the jungle.

Emotions racked her body as she pressed onward and broke down in choking sobs. Captain Scarlett ordered Connell to collect the panther's body and then chased after Elaine. He could not let her leave without saying goodbye. He must see her again, even if it killed him.

"Elaine!" Captain Scarlett placed one foot in front of the other, as his heart pounded against his chest. She was fast, but he had to be faster. He had to catch her. "Elaine!"

Looking back at him, Elaine caught her breath and ran. She raced through the trees as her arms swiped through the air around her. She felt sick and nauseous, loose bile rising at the back of her throat. But she had to be away from him and killing and blood and death.

"Elaine!" Captain Scarlett caught sight of her up ahead and picked up his pace.

Her thighs burned with discomfort as she charged forward, but Captain Scarlett wanted to reach her more than she wanted to flee. For that reason, he reached out and grabbed her arm, pulling her back to him.

Elaine cried and buried her face in her hands. But Captain Scarlett took off his hat and reached out to stroke her chin. Then he leaned in and kissed her. Still weak and trembling, Elaine lacked the capacity to move, so he clutched her arms and cupped her face tenderly within the palm of his hand. Crushing his mouth to hers, Captain Scarlett coaxed her lips apart and took every bit of pleasure from her that she would allow.

Deep down, he knew that he had taken advantage of the woman, shaken from the killing of the panther and emotional with the newly discovered pregnancy. But he could not keep himself from tasting her one last time. Because he knew it was a chance that he would never have again.

Captain Scarlett touched his lips to hers a final time and broke away for air. As he cradled Elaine's face in his hands, she gazed up at him with tears in her eyes. Pain stabbed him in the chest, for she had merely kept still as payment for her ultimate freedom and release was made.

"Let me go," she begged. "I want my husband. I need my husband."

Captain Scarlett's hands fell away from her face as he stared at her one last time. "Yes." He nodded and pinned his dark brows together in pain. "You may go." He waved an arm and motioned in the direction away from the group of men. "No one will follow you."

Elaine dried her tears and sobbed. "Thank you." Shaking with relief, she wrapped her arms around his body and gave him a tight squeeze. "Thank you," she whispered.

Captain Scarlett pulled away and braced her

shoulders. "Go on," he directed.

She smiled and left an innocent kiss on his cheek. Then she grabbed the skirt of her gown and ran off into the jungle. Just before she disappeared from view, Elaine turned back to Captain Scarlett and let him look at her one last time.

Chapter 18

Tearing through the jungle, Elaine ran as far as her feet would carry her. Wind blew through her hair and cut against her face with every valiant hurdle and leap. Before long, she reached the edge of the jungle where Henry was there looking out at the horizon. In her mind, they shared a spiritual sort of communication, and he had been waiting for her.

"Henry!" Elaine cried out, rushing towards him.

Henry turned around and Elaine sailed into his arms, nearly tackling him to the ground with the way she jumped on top of him. Drawing her into his embrace, Henry smelled her hair and kissed her face. Then he held her at arm's length and looked over her.

"Are you all right, my love?" He brushed the pad of his thumb against her cheekbone and inspected her body for damage or injury. "Did they harm you?"

"No," she cooed, grappling with the fabric of his shirt. "I am free."

When Elaine burst into tears, Henry clutched her head and pulled her close. Frederic and Louisa appeared with a pair of wide eyes, glancing from Henry to Elaine. He held up a hand in understanding and rubbed Elaine's back as she buried her head in his chest.

"Oh, thank God," Louisa sighed with relief.

By the look on his face, it was clear that Frederic shared the sentiment.

Elaine lifted her head from Henry's chest and looked up, spotting the visitors. She rushed over to Louisa and gave her a hug, glad that she was safe, glad that she was all right, glad that her attempt at saving the poor girl and sacrificing herself had not been all for nothing.

While Louisa comforted Elaine, she looked over her shoulder for an instant and found Judas sneaking up with a pistol in his hand. He was drenched in water, soaking wet, his head shaking with fury and vengeance. The vein across his forehead nearly popped.

"Henry!" Louisa cried, for his back was to Judas.

Turning around in a flash, Henry drew his dagger and moved towards Frederic, Elaine and Louisa. The men huddled together and forced the women behind them out of an innate drive to protect them. But Judas stalked closer and held the gun with a shaky hand.

"I want my treasure," Judas shivered, practically maniacal. "Where is it?"

Frederic stepped in and answered, "We have already shown you."

"A mere piece of gold?" Judas snapped back. "You truly expect me to believe that is all there was at the bottom of that spring?"

Henry clenched his fist and Elaine swallowed, while Frederic and Louisa hardly moved an inch.

"One of you has taken it," Judas decided. "I'm just not sure which one."

"We do not have it and we do not know what has happened to it," Louisa spoke up, feigning bravery. Less of a challenge with Frederic around. "I swear."

Judas cocked his brow and took a step towards her. "Why dear Louisa, I have never known of you, even during our courtship, to swear."

She turned red at the sound of his words, even though she had done no more than speak the truth. Even with the four of them, she could not escape her fear of Judas. There was something about him that always resulted in the outcome of his victory.

"Perhaps it is in the possession of Captain Scarlett," Elaine butted in.

Henry looked to her in confusion, but she kept her eyes on Judas.

"What?" Judas narrowed his eyes in distrust.

"Are you not acquainted with him? With Captain Gregory Scarlett?"

Judas blinked several times until she stood before him and lowered his gun.

"What are you playing at?" Judas responded, watching her every breath.

"Yes, Ms. Carmichael." Captain Scarlett appeared through the trees. "What are you playing at?" As he stood behind Judas, Connell and the guard fanned out beside him. The last to come hobbling over was the elderly man in chains. He nearly fell down on his journey to reach them.

"Father!" Frederic hurried over and knelt down before the old man. He reached out and hugged his father, fragile and shaking in the chains. He was practically skin and bones.

"It was you," Elaine realized. She flitted her eyes over to Captain Scarlett with a scowl. "You are the one Judas hired to hold Frederic's father prisoner?"

"I am not proud of my actions, Ms. Carmichael. But yes."

Fuming with rage, Elaine marched towards Captain Scarlett and struck him across the face. Then she glowered into his dark eyes and spit in his face. "You are a coward."

Captain Scarlett smirked down at her then pulled out a pistol and pointed it at Frederic's father. "Get up!" he shouted at Frederic. "Get up! Now!"

Trembling with fear, Frederic backed away and crumpled to the ground. All this time, he had been hanging on to a thread of hope that his father might still be alive. Now that they had finally been reunited, the bloody pirates were going to kill him anyway.

Sensing danger, Henry reached out and held Elaine to shield her from harm's way. But in the process, Judas grabbed ahold of Louisa and tugged at her hair. She let out a screeching cry as Frederic, Elaine, and Henry looked back in shock.

"You must make a choice, Frederic," Judas snarled as he pressed the end of the pistol to Louisa's head. She was frantic and trembling, looking out at her loved ones with tears in her eyes.

"Yes," Captain Scarlett insisted. "Your father or her."

"What? NO!" Frederic ripped his fingers through his auburn hair in agony.

Henry and Elaine jumped up to provide some defense, but Connell and the guard already had their rifles in the air aimed at either of them. Despite four, they were simply outnumbered. Frederic had never anticipated Judsa would have such allies as this.

"Let the girl go," the old man said. It was the first time Elaine had ever heard him speak. Now that she had, she could not believe she had failed to make the connection before. Despite his thinning white hair, the man had unmistakable gray eyes. The same that belonged to Frederic.

"But, Father," Frederic whimpered, wet tears stinging his eyes.

"I am old and weak," Frederic's father declared. "She is young and full of beauty. Her whole life ahead of her. Let her live. Choose me. It is what is best."

"All right, sir," Captain Scarlett declared. "As you wish."

"Father! No!" Frederic cried out, lunging forward despite the guns drawn at him.

Captain Scarlett pressed the pistol to the old man's head. Utterly calm, Frederic's father closed his eyes as if he were already at peace with his destiny. But before Captain Scarlett could pull the trigger, in a lithe, cat-like move, he turned the gun on Judas and fired.

The bullet pierced his neck as Judas stumbled backward and fell to the flat of his back on the hard ground. While the entire party fell into silence, Captain Scarlett brought the elderly man to his feet and pushed him towards the shore. "GO!" he barked, motioning to the rest of his crew. "GO! RUN!" he shouted to Frederic and Louisa who took off after his father. Elaine shared a glance with Captain Scarlett before Henry grabbed her arm and dragged her away.

When there were two men remaining, Captain Scarlett slowly stalked towards Judas. His head dug into the ground as he choked on his own blood, shaking with convulsions. Captain Scarlett clenched his jaw and sucked his cheeks inward, standing over the man in a taunting manner.

"Gregory," Judas coughed. "You know me.

We are the same. You and I."

Captain Scarlett smiled and raised his pistol. "No. We are not."

Judas squeezed his eyes shut and clamped his hand around his arm to cope with the agony. "Gregory, dear God don't!" He shook with fright, even though he must have anticipated that death was surely on its way. "Brother, please!" he whimpered.

"You are not my brother," Captain Scarlett answered. "Not anymore."

Lowering his weapon, Captain Scarlett looked over the life of his younger brother for the last time. In the past, they had shared the same mother, but that was another life. Similar blood may have run through their veins, but not the kind Captain Scarlett desired to have.

"Brother! Don't leave me! Please don't leave me to die in the jungle!"

Ignoring his words, Captain Scarlett turned his back on Judas and walked away.

As he became to bleed out, Judas felt the life pulsing from his veins, as if some greater force was sucking every part of him away. Strength was out of his grasp, but he fought through the turmoil in an attempt to hold on. But then something flickered out of the corner of his eye, and Judas became paralyzed with fear at the sight.

A beautiful black panther stalked towards him with vengeance in her fiery green eyes. Judas raised his arms in the air and flailed about, rocking from side to side to get his body off the ground. But the big cat staked her claim and placed her paw over his chest.

Razor sharp claws retracted from her toes as she swiped them against his flesh again and again. Judas screamed and cried as blood spattered everywhere, flying into his eyes, but no one was coming to his rescue. To quicken the death, the panther opened her wide jaws and sank her fangs into the side of Judas's neck.

When blood seeped through his clothing, Judas looked up at the green tapestry of the jungle overhead and then closed his eyes. With a final breath, all of the air escaped his lungs and his head fell to the side. Even though she was hungry, the black panther sniffed the dead body to make sure life had inevitably left.

Then the jungle cat glanced over Judas one last time, turned on her heel and left.

Chapter 19

Captain Scarlett raced across the sand and shouted orders for his crew to climb aboard and set sail. Connell and the guard followed his command and began preparing for departure, while the old man in chains wept with tears of joy at the sight of his son. Frederic pulled him into a bear hug and kept Louisa close, not wanting to let either of them ever out of his sight ever again.

"We must leave at once," Captain Scarlett interrupted. Within seconds, he had one of his crewmen freeing Frederic's father of the shackles that had bound him. Along with Frederic and Louisa, they climbed aboard Captain Scarlett's ship with haste.

Henry draped his arm across Elaine's back and pulled her in the same direction, until Captain Scarlett stood in his way. "We are leaving the island," Henry declared. "The same as everyone else."

Captain Scarlett looked from Henry to Elaine

and smiled. "It would be foolish to leave La Fleur Noire on the island." He motioned to the ship once under the ownership of Captain William Pierce. "We will take her back to New York, while everyone else remains on La Fleur Rouge. I thought you would prefer privacy above all else."

Henry shook his head to let everything fully sink in. He was still recovering from the shock of the matter that Captain Scarlett was no ally of Judas but an enemy. His actions had saved them all, and Henry was forever indebted to him for his bravery and kindness.

"Thank you, Captain Scarlett." Henry stuck his hand out for the captain to shake. "You have no idea how grateful my wife and I are for what you have done. Thank you. Truly."

Captain Scarlett shook his hand and then tucked his palms beneath his arms. "Believe me, Mr. Rochester. It was my pleasure." He looked at Elaine and then turned around to walk away.

* * *

Once everyone climbed aboard both ships, La Fleur Noire and La Fleur Rouge set sail for America. Elaine sat by a window below deck with her legs pulled into her chest. She peered through the glass and saw a black panther, her black panther, the black panther with green eyes, walk out onto the sand as they drifted away. At that very moment, Elaine looked back at her with a smile. The truth was startlingly clear. Jade had a daughter.

"How are you, my love?" Henry strolled over to Elaine and touched her back, sensing her sadness.

"All right, Henry." She wiped a lonesome teardrop away and sighed. "It's just hard. Leaving all over again. I feel as though a part of me will be lost forever."

Henry leaned over her shoulder to grasp her hand. Feeling a sense of loss, she turned back to Henry and gazed up at him. When he clutched her chin in his hand, she shivered and shut her eyes. Then he traced the edge of her jawline with his finger and touched her neck.

"I'm pregnant," she whispered, letting the words roll sweetly off her tongue.

Henry stilled at the sound of her words, his lips parting slightly. "What?"

"Yes." She nodded. "We're having another baby."

His jaw dropped wide open until he smiled like the happiest man in the world. Wrapping his arms around her, Henry picked Elaine up and spun her around. She giggled with delight at his reaction and bit her lip when he set her feet back on the ground.

Without a moment to waste, Henry grabbed her waist and pushed her back into the wall. Elaine let out a sigh of contentment as his lips forged a path down her neck. Clinging to the fabric of his shirt, Elaine rolled her head to the side as her breathing increased.

"I love you, Elaine," Henry gasped, tugging at the folds of her dress.

"And I love you," she answered back, equally breathless.

After being parted from her for so long, Henry turned her around and unfastened the buttons descending the length of her spine. He swept her black locks to the side and planted a soft kiss against the back of her neck, helping her out of the dress. As he peeled the sleeves back to reveal her skin, Henry ran his nose along her throat and inhaled.

Elaine lifted her arms and wrapped her hands around her husband, desperate to have him near. Once her dress hit the floor, Elaine pushed Henry against the opposite wall and began unfastening the buttons on his shirt. He took her face in his hands and molded his mouth to hers, relaxing as she freed him from the rest of his clothing and chucked it to the floor.

Henry trailed his fingertips down her naked back and picked her up in his arms, carrying her to the cot by the wall. When her body made contact with the soft bedding, Elaine reached out and clung to Henry until he came closer. He folded his fingers through hers and consumed her mouth as her nails pierced his back, scratching and scraping.

When Elaine gasped, Henry covered her mouth with a demanding kiss and buried his face in her neck. She wrapped Henry in her arms and glowed with warmth at the feeling of having him all around her again. Somehow, they had overcome the jungle a second time and made it out alive. Now they were headed back to New York to greet their darling little Lilly with the prospect of a new one on the way.

As Henry brushed his lips against hers, she smiled at every kiss and treasured every touch. Deep down, she had the feeling that they would never be separated again. No one would ever come between them, because theirs was a love that lasts a lifetime.

* * *

Captain Scarlett gazed up at the moonlight from the deck, steering the ship alone in the night. After several swigs of rum, he was nursing the dull ache in his heart. Elaine had been reunited with her husband, and he was happy that she was happy. But pain remained for the love he could never get from her, because it had already been given away.

He looked across the way at La Fleur Noire. Connell waved to him from the deck, where he was steering the ship straight ahead. Side by side, they rode across the ocean in the night, more able to protect each other as a fleet rather than as individual ships. But then he caught sight of Frederic twirling young Louisa around in a circle and his heartache ensued. How could it be that everyone on the island had found love but him?

Then again, that was not entirely true. He had found love on the island.

Just with the wife of another man.

* * *

After a week at sea, Elaine crept up the staircase one night when she couldn't sleep. Henry had dozed off hours ago, but something seemed to be troubling her mind. So she climbed up to the deck and found Captain Scarlett steering the ship all by his lonesome.

In a way, Elaine felt guilty for leaving the full responsibility of taking them home on Gregory's shoulders. After all, he had already done so much for them. Elaine felt sure that she knew the only reason why. It was an attempt to reclaim his soul and reform himself.

"Mrs. Rochester," Captain Scarlett greeted, tipping his hat in her direction.

She eyed the ruby red feather and wondered at the significance. Surely, there must have been some story there, but she was not nosey enough to ask. "Good evening."

Captain Scarlett kept an eye on the horizon as the pearly moon hung overhead. Feeling a cool breeze drift across the deck, Elaine took a seat near the edge and admired all of the natural beauty around her that would soon be gone forever. "Are you feeling well?"

Elaine looked over in confusion and then

touched her stomach. "Yes. Thank you for asking."

"Have you told Henry the wonderful news?" he wondered, looking ahead.

"Yes." She nodded and stared out at the waves with a grin. "He is thrilled."

"As he should be," was Captain Scarlett's only reply. Some time passed, in which he did more staring at the sight of Elaine than he should have. "Will you miss it?" he asked.

She draped a protective arm across her stomach without even realizing it. Scanning his profile, she furrowed her brow in all seriousness. "Miss what?"

"All of this." He gestured out at the great blue sea. "The island. The jungle."

Elaine dropped her eyes to the deck and then gazed out at the ocean. "Yes. There are things I will miss. And there are things I will not," she confessed.

Captain Scarlett tightened his grip on the wheel and clenched his jaw. He desperately wanted to know which group he belonged to, hoping it was not the latter.

"What about you?" Elaine pressed. "What is next in the enviable life of Gregory Scarlett, Captain of La Fleur Rouge?" She smiled merely out of politeness, but he wished it had meant more.

"Well, I plan to return to London. I will decide my next move there."

"And what of them?" Elaine dropped her face in pity. Though she had been cryptic, he knew the meaning behind her question. She spoke of the leopard and panther. "What will happen to them, Gregory?"

The way she said his name sent tingles straight to his fingertips, but he pushed them aside and focused on the crushing waves in the distance. "They will be skinned or stuffed."

Elaine gulped and nodded her head in understanding. "I see."

"I'll have you know that ours was my last hunt. I'm giving it up, Elaine."

"What?" She braided her fingers together and glanced over him as if she hadn't heard him correctly.

"I am tired of traveling to faraway lands and traipsing through the wilderness. I believe my future is in weaponry, ammunition, things of that sort."

"There is good business in the gun trade?" she wondered.

"Why, of course," he replied. "We are bound to have another war. If not two."

Elaine lowered her lashes and let his words sink in. Somehow, without any understanding as to how, she knew that he was right. She knew that it would happen.

"Who are you?" Elaine wondered.

"I am no one really, Ms. Carmichael. Just an old friend sent to help."

Utterly perplexed, Elaine rose to her feet and approached him. "Have we met? Why do I feel like I know you?" Her eyes flitted over his features, as she gazed into those dark eyes, sometimes black as night, other times like warm golden honey, as they were now.

"You are mistaken, Ms. Carmichael. I can assure you. I wish you and Henry the best."

Taking the hint, Elaine flushed at the realization that he was asking her to leave.

"Thank you, Gregory." She shivered at the chill and detected sadness in his eyes. Even though he was no more than a friend, she wondered if she had been the one to cause it.

As Elaine walked away and descended the staircase where she could join her husband in bed below deck, Captain Scarlett forced the thick lump down his throat. When the door closed, and he knew that she was gone for the night, he stepped away from the wheel. Then he scrambled above deck and searched for the first bottle of rum he could find.

Chapter 20

Frederic relaxed on the deck of the ship with his father by his side, telling stories and making him laugh like he used to. Louisa sat beside Frederic, just as amused by his father's dry humor and quick wit. Now that his father had been set free, Frederic could set out to live the life he so chose. Not one that had been decided for him.

"I believe I should go rest," Frederic's father announced. He gave his son a hug and then turned to Louisa and tenderly took her palm. "It was lovely to meet you, dear."

"You as well." She smiled up at him without showing any teeth, a natural rosy hue to her cheeks. When he stood up and took a slow time walking away, the motion tugged at her heartstrings. All the time he had been held captive had caught up with him.

La Fleur Rouge cut the surface of the water, breaking waves as they surged on into the night.

Grateful for small blessings, Louisa was fortunate enough to have Frederic all to herself. With all of the other men asleep below deck, it was just the two of them out in the moonlight.

When Louisa looked at Frederic, his eyes were on the horizon. She turned her head to follow his line of sight, but could not understand why it felt like he was ignoring her. Desperate to break the silence, she leaned closer until her arm brushed against his.

"Can you believe it, Frederic? We are going home," she chimed.

By the time Frederic met her gaze, there was hardly any trace of a smile left on his face. "Yes, Louisa. We are." He faked an expression of pleasure, but she saw straight through the false exterior.

"Captain Scarlett said that by the time we arrive, it might be Christmas," she noted.

"Is that so?" Frederic crossed his arms over his chest, showing no intention of wanting to touch her. The realization pained Louisa's heart, because she could not understand why he appeared so cold towards her. They had escaped death. They had escaped the island. They were going home. Shouldn't he have been more excited over the matter?

"Yes, darling." She placed her hand on his shoulder and leaned in for a kiss. But Frederic shot her a wayward glance that could have killed. So she retracted her palm and leaned back, worrying over what she must have done wrong.

Frederic parted his lips to speak, though no words came out. Emotions raced across his face, developing every feature into something else altogether. Louisa could not decipher if he were angry, sad, anxious, or some combination of the three.

"What are your plans once we arrive in New York?" Louisa kept herself from tacking my love onto the end of the question, because she had a feeling he might not like it. Now that they were out of the jungle, Frederic Holmes had become an entirely new person.

Frederic lowered his gaze and exhaled aloud, as if she were too much trouble to bother answering. Then he drummed his fingers over his thigh and ignored her completely.

"You were just so talkative before," she reminded him, pointing in the direction his father had just gone. "Why won't you speak to me? What have I done to offend you?"

With the shake of his head, Frederic ran a hand over his beard and finally said, "Nothing."

Pondering his dull answer for a moment, Louisa folded her palms over her lap as if she were about to say a prayer. Had she not been kind enough to his father? The old man was delightful and funny, traits which she hoped to see in Frederic one day.

"Have I said something?" Louisa wondered. When he made no reply, she carried on with more questions. "I thought you would be happy returning to America?"

"I am happy," he bluntly stated, sharp and quick. Like the edge of a knife.

"Oh, I see." Louisa lowered her gaze to keep from revealing the sadness in her eyes. "You are happy to return home to America. Just not with me. Is that it?"

Blowing hot air through his nostrils, Frederic shifted to face her and scowled. "Why must you be such a fool? Have you no concept of life? Of reality? Of the world?"

Taken aback by his words, Louise squared her shoulders until her posture became more rigid and straight. "Of course I do," she fired back. "Why do you think me a fool?"

"I must sort my life out, Louisa," he affirmed. "I have made a mess of things, and there is no way of fixing the matter. I must find decent work and a home. I need to be able to take care of my father."

Louisa nibbled on the edge of her lip and considered how she could help. "I am sure Henry could provide work. We have a family business and the factory burned down. When we return, I am sure one of the first things Henry will see to is having it rebuilt. And then he will need help with running the business and—"

"No," he coldly remarked. "I will not take charity from some rich girl."

Fighting the lump in her throat, Louisa lowered her voice and shuddered. "Why do you hate me so?" She fluttered her dark lashes, but the tears came just as effortlessly.

"You must understand, Louisa. You are too young to realize the way the world works."

Letting his words sink in, Louisa turned her back to him and dried her eyes. It was clear to see that it was happening all over again. He was severing all ties and breaking her heart.

"Yes, Frederic," she eventually said. "You are right. I just thought things would be different in New York. You are planning on staying in New York? Aren't you?"

When Louisa looked back at him, Frederic smoldered and rubbed his palms against one another. "I will go wherever I find the best opportunity. For me and my father."

"I see," she said, feeling like quicksand on the inside. "You have no plans to stay."

Frederic dared to look over, even though he had been forcing himself to turn his gaze elsewhere. It was merely too painful to look at her, when he knew the way it would all end eventually. It was the way it was supposed to end. The way it had always been planned to end. It was their destiny.

"Louisa." He cupped her cheek in his palm and wiped a fresh tear away. "I am not cut out for the life of your husband. We are not suited for each other."

She mashed her lips together and turned her face into the warmth of his skin.

"I am thinking of you, as well," he mentioned, turning sweet and tender at the last.

"How so?" Her lower lip quivered as she trembled with grief.

"Well, you are just sixteen." He stroked his fingers through her long blonde hair and touched her skin with a gentle caress. "You have your whole life ahead of you. Why, it has hardly even begun. There is a great big world out there that you have yet to discover."

She sobbed and blinked rapidly so she could make out his face through her tears. "But I want to discover it with you. I want to go wherever you go. I want to be with you."

"My darling girl," Frederic crooned with a smile. "You wouldn't be able to stand me for a minute. And Father, well... let's just say his evening jokes tire with age."

"You know that is not true." She shook her head and leaned in closer. "Why are you always trying to destroy us? Why are you always trying to tear us apart?"

Frederic scanned his eyes over her face and said, "Because it is what's best for you."

Sadness morphed into anger, as Louisa batted his hands away from her face. "What about what happened between us in the forest? Was it real? Even for a moment?"

Frederic bowed his head and looked up, though not at her. "Yes, Louisa. It was real."

"So you still love me?" She motioned to her

heart, hardly noticing the significance.

"Why, of course." Frederic cradled her face in his hands. "Always."

"Just as I love you?" she inquired, searching deep into his silvery eyes.

"Yes," he whispered, glancing from her eyes to her mouth.

"I love you. You love me. So tell me why it is that we cannot be together?"

Frederic pressed his thumb against the bottom of her chin and sighed. "Because love is not enough."

As another crack formed in her already broken heart, Louisa backed away from him and got to her feet. After the emotion of surviving the jungle, she had been elevated with the glorifying feeling of having Frederic in her life. But now all that was gone, crumbling away like pieces of stale, dry bread. She would have rather stayed in the jungle.

When Louisa reached the edge, she positioned her hands on the railing and gazed out into the distance from her place on the ship. Worried that he had betrayed his love, Frederic slowly rose to his feet and followed her. Once he stood behind her, Louisa tensed at the feel of him close by and wiped the back of her hand across her nose.

"Louisa, you must understand. My time with you on the island has been a dream, an illusion, a false reality. I would give anything to make it last. But that is not how the world works. I treasured every moment with you, because I knew a day would come when it would be the last."

Biting her lip, Louisa shut her eyes and took a series of deep, staggering breaths. The absurdity of the whole affair was that they would still be on the ship together for months before they reached America. Why separate now? Surely, they should squeeze the life out of every moment they had left together. But all Frederic wished to do was end the romance prematurely, perhaps to lessen the pain once they finally arrived.

"You have done this once before, Frederic. And I won't let you do it again."

Frederic pinned his brows together at her words, watching her golden blonde hair billow out beneath the moonlight. He reached a hand out to touch her, but then thought twice about it and withdrew. Clenching his hand into a fist, he reminded himself that it would be easier for them both later if he broke it off now. Simply planning for the days ahead.

"If you truly wish to be parted from me, then that is it. When we arrive in New York, you will never see my face again. Is that truly what you desire?" Louisa angled her head to the side but did not turn all the way around to face him. She couldn't bear the look on his face as he thought of his answer. She couldn't bear the look on his face when he saw the tears in her eyes. She couldn't bear the look on his face now.

"Yes," Frederic uttered, though the sound seemed to be trapped at the back of his throat.

Devastated, Louisa turned and fled without giving him a final glance. Her body shook with emotion the moment she sailed downstairs and was far enough away to prevent him from seeing the pain he had caused her. She covered her mouth to stifle the agonizing sound of her sobs and sank down to the ground.

Alone on deck, Frederic inched forward and rested his hand over the railing where she had just been resting hers. Then he looked out at the ocean and the moon overhead. All the same wonders she had just been looking at. When a drop of water hit the wooden railing, he looked down at it and inhaled. There were heavy wet tears in his eyes. And they showed no sign of going away anytime soon.

Chapter 21

S now was falling in New York when Captain Scarlett steered La Fleur Noire up to the docks. Henry and Elaine looked out at the familiar territory around them and felt immediate déjà vu. The moment they had seen the Statue of Liberty, Elaine's skin tingled and flushed with the feeling of going through these motions before, as they had indeed been in the very same place exactly one year ago.

As soon as Henry stepped onto the docks and pulled Elaine alongside him, Captain Scarlett followed closely behind, though only for a moment. Wanting to be gracious, he patted Henry on the back until the young Rochester turned around to see that Captain Scarlett was not headed in the same direction as they were. He was headed home.

"Mr. and Mrs. Rochester?" Captain Scarlett removed his hat and looked from one face to the next. "I wish you both the best."

"Off so soon?" Henry wondered. "Surely, we can offer you a place to stay, at least until you get your feet on the ground and plan your next move."

"No. Thank you, but no." Captain Scarlett waved his hand at the generous offer. "There are places I must be. I have no time for dallying around in New York."

"If you are ever in New York, please stop by for a visit. We should be delighted to see you." Henry stuck out his hand and Captain Scarlett shook it with a grin.

"Thank you, sir. You are very kind." Captain Scarlett slipped his hat back on his head as the red feather blew through the wind. "Mrs. Rochester." He took her palm in his and felt of the delicate skin. Perhaps he would be more jealous if Henry weren't such a decent man, if she weren't actually in love with him. But Elaine was happy, and that was all that mattered. He pressed his lips to the back of her hand and a healthy blush returned to Elaine's cheeks.

"Goodbye, Captain Scarlett," she sweetly crooned. The sound of her voice was like music to his ears, which made it all the more difficult to let her go. In the end, he did let her go though, because it was the right thing to do—it was what she wanted.

"Goodbye, Ms. Carmichael." He turned on his heel and climbed aboard the ship, wasting no time in his departure. As he sailed away into drifting flecks of snow from the sky above, it took every fiber of his being to keep him from looking back at her angelic face, her raven black hair, her glistening green eyes.

But he knew how much pain loving her had already caused him, so he tried to look ahead to the future and focus on that instead. As he steered the ship into the night, Captain Scarlett could have sworn that he felt someone watching him from afar.

He did not look back.

* * *

Louisa stood at the end of the dock and watched Captain Scarlett fade away. She found it odd that he would leave his own ship in lieu of another, but it belonged to no one now that Judas was dead. Somehow, his death did not cause her as much pain as she would have anticipated. Parting with Frederic proved to be much worse.

While she had cared for Captain William Pierce, those feelings were nothing compared to the way she longed for Frederic Holmes. Judas had been an infatuation, a crush, a too-good-to-be-true that she should have realized was just that. But Frederic was the first to truly claim her heart. Judas had been a fantasy, but Frederic was the real deal. Only now, in the real world where men like Frederic exist, he did not want her.

Lingering on the edge of the dock, Louisa wrung her hands together until Frederic looked back over his shoulder at her. After leaving his father on the ship, Frederic stepped off and met Louisa on the dock. Like always, she was waiting for him.

"Hello, Frederic." She inched closer, as he kept an invisible distance between them.

"Hello." He offered a faint smile, one which he was surprised to see that she returned.

"I see that your father is still aboard the ship. Does he not have plans to leave it?"

"No," he muttered. "And neither do I."

"Won't you at least visit? Stay a few days and see the city," she pressed.

"No. A man in the crew has offered me a job. We are leaving for England immediately. I don't have any plans of coming back to America. At least for a while."

Accepting the devastating blow, Louisa forced a smile to make the best of it.

"If matters were different, I can assure you that I would—"

"What? That you would want to be with me? That you would stay because you couldn't bear to leave? That you would actually love me?"

Frederic stole away her gaze and inched closer, until there was hardly an inch of breath left between them. "Don't, for one moment believe that I do not love you."

"If you did, you would never treat me this way. You would never abandon me and leave. You would never want to leave."

"Whoever said that I want to leave?" Frederic took her face in his hands and lifted it up to meet his. "You are the loveliest girl I have ever known. And I will miss you greatly."

Breaking down, Louisa buried her face in Frederic's chest and wrapped her arms around him. With tears in his eyes, Frederic rubbed her back and wished everything were different. As he held her close and squeezed her tight as she cried, Frederic inhaled her scent one last time. It was something he would need to commit to memory, so he may reflect on it and remember for years to come.

When someone shouted for Frederic to climb aboard the ship, his heart sank at the realization that they were ready to depart. Panic flitted across Louisa's face at the sound. So Frederic offered her one last look to spare her the agony.

Then he took her face in his hands and claimed her mouth. It was a passionate, soul-stirring kiss that would remain with her for a lifetime. Gently stroking her arms, Frederic molded his mouth to hers as if their lips were destined to never part. But when he broke away for air, their time was up.

"Goodbye, my love," he uttered, placing a tender kiss on her forehead.

As he left her shuddering with grief, Louisa looked up and watched him walk away. Once he boarded the ship and sailed off, her mouth quivered at the stabbing, aching pain in her chest.

"Goodbye, my love," she whispered. "Goodbye."

Chapter 22

Strolling the streets of New York lacked the same vigor as evenings of the past on that chilly December night. Henry took Elaine's hand as they approached the Rochester Mansion, utterly deserted and abandoned. When Henry opened the door and led Elaine inside, her eyes widened at the discovery that the house had been vandalized.

With his mother and father deceased, the door must have been left hanging wide open for the entirety of his absence. Of course the mansion had been a target for criminals passing by. Only a fool would spot an open treasure chest and not look inside.

Elaine walked into the drawing room and sat down on the sofa, recalling her talk with Louisa in this very room before the naïve young girl left in search of William. More than six months had passed since that fateful night, yet it seemed like a lifetime ago. Then again, when Elaine reflected on their return to the island, it felt like it had happened yesterday.

When Henry was brave enough to climb the staircase on his own, he took them two at a time until he reached the top. Bracing himself for the smell, Henry pushed the door open to the master bedroom to find that his mother's body was missing. As he stepped further into the room, Henry looked from left to right until the truth inevitably set in.

They must have proceeded through the funerals without him.

Unable to bear the hole in his heart, Henry retreated and closed the door behind him. He walked into the hallway and slipped his hands in his pockets, understanding that time had not stopped while they were away on the island. Somehow, he had envisioned a scenario where New York remained frozen in time, waiting for them to return before another second ticked by. But Henry was wrong. The whole world had carried on without them.

When Henry climbed back down the staircase, he found Elaine and they walked through the rest of the mansion before reaching the cellar where he had locked her up. The door was still split down the middle with that gaping hole at the center, as if a beast had burrowed its way inside. In truth, the beast had been more animal than human.

Feeling brave, Henry unlocked his fingers from Elaine's and weaved his way through the rest of the mansion alone. In the long corridor leading to his father's study, Henry stopped in his tracks and swallowed down the lump forming in his throat. He lowered his head and placed one foot in front of the other, his heart thrumming with a wild rhythm.

Henry opened the door and stepped inside, surprised to find that all of Mr. Rochester's possessions had remained untouched. In fact, it may have been the only room in the mansion that had retained the appearance of what it had once looked like. Henry observed the documents on his father's desk, ink and parchment. Then he walked over and took a seat in his chair, hoping to absorb the essence of his father that had been left behind in the room. Even with Mr. Rochester gone, Henry could feel his spirit all around him, like a soft cloth blanketing him with warmth and unconditional love.

On her own, Elaine ambled into the billiard room and shut the door. In all her time at the Rochester Mansion, she couldn't remember ever stepping in here before. So she walked over a mess of shattered glass and approached the billiard table. Lost in the strange world she had once called home, Elaine picked up the eight ball and then dropped it down onto the green felt, listening as it knocked against two solids.

When something caught her eye, Elaine walked around the billiard table and found a framed photograph of Henry and another man, perhaps a companion. He had curly hair and a pleasant enough smile, which made Elaine wonder why she had never heard of him before. Removing the photo from the frame, Elaine tucked it into the palm of her hand and set out to find Henry.

After traveling through the mansion alone, Elaine knocked on the half-open door to Mr. Rochester's study and found Henry sitting at the desk inside. With a forced smile, she stepped in and took a seat in the chair across from the desk. Despite the absence of tears in his eyes, Elaine could see that Henry was hurting. Even though they had escaped the island and ultimately survived for a second time, it seemed as if there was nothing to return to but loss and regret.

Mr. and Mrs. Rochester were still gone.

"I found this photograph," Elaine mentioned. She handed the picture to him across the desk and noted the furrow of his brow. "Who is that man, Henry? Why haven't I ever met him before?"

Henry set the picture down and cleared his throat. "He was a close friend of mine." His eyes remained down, as his mind traveled back to the night Charlie had convinced him to join the voyage across the Atlantic.

"What was his name?" Elaine wondered, searching his tired face.

"Charles Gallagher," Henry replied. "I suppose I should thank him for meeting you."

Elaine pinned her black brows together and parted her lips to ask why.

"It was Charles who insisted that I join the crew of men sailing across the Atlantic. I never imagined that I would be the only one on board to survive."

Elaine pressed her lips together and studied him carefully, longing to ease his affliction.

"He drowned along with all of the other men, Elaine. But I washed ashore and met you on the island instead. I owe my whole life to that man." Henry pointed at the photograph.

"As do I," Elaine mused. After all, had Henry never been stranded the same as Elaine, she would have been trapped on that island forever. Even in death, Charles Gallagher had brought them life.

"We must go home." Henry lifted his eyes to Elaine, as she nodded with tears in her eyes.

When Henry turned in his father's chair and opened his arms wide, Elaine walked around the desk and sat down in his lap. Henry cradled her body close as she wrapped her hands at the nape of his neck, gazing down at him despite blurry, tear-filled eyes. He touched the edge of her chin and acknowledged her stomach, placing his hand over the flat surface that would soon become a round bump.

Elaine rested her hands on his shoulders and leaned in for a soft kiss. Henry returned the sweet gesture and touched his lips to hers. Then they sat together for the longest time, as Elaine sank into the warmth of his embrace and put her head on his chest.

Henry stroked his fingers through her hair and rubbed her back as she squeezed him tight. Taking slow, deep breaths, Elaine clutched the fabric of his shirt and embraced all of the good that remained in their lives. The good that had unfortunately come with the death of loved ones who they would never be able to see again.

* * *

When Henry and Elaine stepped outside, they found Louisa crying on the front doorsteps. Her face was buried in her hands as her entire body shook with violent sobs.

"I'll take care of this, Henry," Elaine volunteered. "You just find someone to take us home."

Henry nodded and kissed her on the forehead. Then he left the walkway and searched for a carriage in the night. Elaine watched him go and looked down at his young sister.

"He's gone," Louisa whimpered. She lifted her face to look up at her sister-in-law. "Frederic is gone." Shiny tears streamed down her cheeks as she wept.

Taking a seat beside her, Elaine brushed the hair over Louisa's shoulder and then pulled her into a comforting embrace. For a moment, Louisa sat there shaking and crying as Elaine did her best to console her. The separation from Frederic was so excruciating that she was in physical pain.

"Where has he gone?" Elaine wondered,

remaining calm and kind.

"London," Louisa muttered. "He said that he must make a life of his own and take care of his father. But I never imagined that life would not include me."

"I know, Louisa," Elaine gently consoled. "I know."

As she grabbed ahold of herself and shivered at the falling snow, Louisa looked out at the harbor and wished to turn back the clock. If it were possible, she knew that she would relive this one night with him over and over again, even if it meant that they were trapped in the past for an eternity. It was the only way they could be together.

"Do you think I will ever see him again?" Louisa glanced up at Elaine and dried her eyes. She felt weak and drained of life, prepared to crawl into her bed and die.

Wanting to be honest with the girl, Elaine parted her lips and sighed. "I don't know."

Louisa nodded, her entire body trembling as it racked her with pain to the core.

In no time at all, Henry arrived with a driver and carriage.

"You cannot stay here alone, Louisa," Elaine said. "Come with us to the country. It will be a chance for you to escape now that we are back in the city. We will take care of you."

Louisa followed the advice of Henry and Elaine and let them guide her to the carriage.

Once she climbed inside, Louisa leaned her head against the door and stared out the window. The farther the horses carried them from the docks, the deeper the separation grew between her and Frederic. As he moved farther to London and she moved farther into the country.

On the journey home, Elaine placed her head in Henry's lap as they all looked out the glass pane and fell into a state of silence. It was still such a shock, all that they had gone through in the jungle, all that they had survived. It seemed too good to be true.

The fear remained that it had yet to end, that Judas would come popping back up at any given moment. Elaine prayed that he was dead for good, that this time it would stick.

* * *

When the carriage reached their home in the country, Elaine leapt out and beat against the front door until Martha answered it. She leapt into the arms of their most trusted house servant and then tore through the place in an attempt to make it upstairs.

"Where is she?" Elaine gasped, choking on tears. "Where is Lilly?"

Martha followed her up to the master bedroom, where Elaine held her palm to her throat at the sight of Lilly sleeping in her crib. By some miracle, her child had survived. She was still alive, though she had grown considerably while they were away.

"Do you think she will remember me?" Elaine approached Lilly and tenderly stroked her fingers against her soft face. "Her hair is so dark," Elaine commented.

"Yes," Martha replied. "She looks like you."

Elaine turned back to Martha with tears in her eyes and then picked Lilly up in her arms. When the baby's eyelids fluttered open, Elaine took a seat in the rocking chair and held Lilly to her breast. Tears skittered down Elaine's face, because she had parted with her daughter for so long that it had almost been impossible to cope.

"And yes," Martha murmured. "Babies know the scent of their mother. She will remember you."

Flooding with warmth at the thought, Elaine cried and pressed her lips to Lilly's forehead. When Henry entered the bedroom, Martha understood the Rochesters' need for privacy and left so the family could have a moment alone together. His eyes connected with Elaine's, as he strode towards his wife and child with joy swelling in his heart.

"My, how she has grown," Henry noted. "May I hold her?"

"Of course," Elaine wept. She stood and gingerly placed Lilly in her father's arms. Smiling with delight, Henry rested her head on his shoulder and patted her back as she drifted off. "Has Martha cared for her all this time? How did she—?"

"I told her to," Henry interrupted. "Before I went to the factory that morning, I left her with enough money for two years and told her to take care of the estate and look after our little girl in case something should happen. I just had a feeling it was the right thing to do."

Breathing through her mouth in relief, Elaine cuddled into Henry's arm and nestled in the warmth of their little family. When Louisa knocked on the door and peeked her head inside, Elaine and Henry turned to find her watching them.

"It is all right, Louisa," Elaine called. "You may come in."

"Yes, Louisa," Henry chimed, holding Lilly close. "Come look at my beautiful daughter."

Louisa entered the room with a sweet smile and stared in awe at her precious niece who had grown in age while they were away. Wanting to show affection, she held out her hand for Lilly as the child squeezed her aunt's fingers with interest. Despite exhaustion, Louisa glanced over the sweet bundle of joy and laughed, her body swelling with warmth.

The Rochesters watched Lilly for what must have been hours as reality dawned on every single one of them. She was worth it. All they had been fighting for.

Chapter 23

When Henry and Elaine were gifted with the birth of a son the following summer, Louisa could not contain her excitement. She bolted up the staircase and grappled with the skirt of her gown, barging in the bedroom door the moment she was allowed. Once she crossed the threshold, Louisa held a palm to her chest to catch her breath.

"Come in, Louisa," Elaine murmured, her forehead slick with sweat.

With the doctor and Martha heading out, Louisa approached the master bed and sat down on the edge. Elaine held a sleeping newborn wrapped in a blue blanket in her arms. When Louisa leaned forward to look at the boy, her spirit expanded with light.

"I am sure he is delighted to meet his Aunt Louisa." Henry patted his sister on the shoulder and looked down at her with a grin. When he turned his golden gaze back on his son, Elaine beamed up at her husband at the ecstasy reflected in both of their eyes.

"What will you call him?" Louisa wondered. "Have you decided on a name?"

Elaine grinned at her curiosity. "Would you like to tell her, Henry?"

"Philip Charles Rochester," Henry revealed. "After Father and Charlie."

Louisa bowed her head in reverence and admired the cooing child. When he burped, Elaine giggled, and it was the sort of laughter that Louisa had never heard from her before.

"He really is beautiful," Louisa declared. "You should both be proud."

"We are, dear sister." Henry crawled across the bed and sat down beside Elaine. Then he placed a kiss on her cheek and gazed down at the beautiful wonder they had created. "We are," he repeated, as the words echoed throughout the room.

"Well, look who we have here," Elaine chimed, a healthy glow to her skin.

Little Lilly toddled in and tumbled to the ground. Hardly a year old, she was just learning how to walk and making a mighty good show of it. With a warm laugh, Louisa slipped down off the bed and ambled over to Lilly. When she picked her niece up in her arms, Louisa returned to the bed and took a seat.

"Mama," Lilly motioned her lips, hardly an utterance from her mouth.

"Would you like to meet your brother?" Elaine asked with a smirk.

Lilly struggled to pull out of her aunt's lap, so Louisa put her down on the bed and watched her crawl the rest of the way to her mother.

"Come here, baby girl." Elaine patted an empty spot on the other side of her. When Lilly reached the spot, Elaine wrapped an arm around her, and she curled into her mother's embrace. "This is your new brother, Philip."

Looking over him in wonder, Lilly watched the baby and kept her eyes readily fixed on his face. As Henry caught Elaine's gaze, he turned her face to his and gifted a soft kiss on her mouth. Then Elaine leaned her head on Henry's shoulder, as they sat in silence to admire the beautiful family they had created amid the throes of love and danger.

"I should leave you alone to celebrate," Louisa suggested.

"Oh," Elaine replied, sounding surprised. "All right."

"Louisa, you are a part of our family, too," Henry reminded her. "You are welcome to stay in here with us. I can assure you that neither of us mind."

"Thank you, but I am feeling rather tired. I'd like to go lie down and rest."

"All right," Henry answered. "As you wish."

"Are you feeling all right?" Elaine wondered. Lilly looked up at her aunt as she got down off the bed and made for the door.

"Yes, I am fine. Just flushed from the summer heat is all."

Henry and Elaine nodded, though both knew there was something Louisa was not telling them. Regardless, she stepped into the hallway and placed one foot in front of the other until she reached her bedroom. Then she breezed through and shut the door behind her, fearfully staring at what lay on her desk by the window.

With a deep breath, she walked across the room and scooped up the thing that had been haunting her dreams for the past several nights. Nearly a week ago, Louisa had received a letter from London, England. A letter addressed to her alone, with a return address for a Mr. Frederic Holmes.

She plopped down in a chair by the window and peered through the glass, toying with the letter in her hands. Why had it been so difficult to open? Surely, whatever he had to say could cause her no more pain than what had already been done.

Tired of wondering and hoping, Louisa ripped the envelope open and fished out the letter that was inside. As she peeled the folded paper back and spread the parchment out on her desk, she noticed black ink in elegant hand. With her heart throbbing, she braced herself for the worst and began to read.

Dearest Louisa,

I know it has been some time since we have spoken. When I left you standing on that dock in New York, I hope you know that it was the hardest decision of my life. But I want you to be happy. And I have no idea how you would be happy with a man like me.

Father developed a terrible case of pneumonia this spring, but he has since made a full recovery. I thank every doctor involved, because I nearly could have lost him again. He speaks of you often, and I tell him that you are living a beautiful life in New York. But perhaps that is deceitful, because I do not know what kind of life you are living in New York.

For Father's sake, I would like to ask, Are you happy?

I have found a job working at a bank here in London. Father and I live together in a flat that I would be ashamed to bring you to, but I know we will not be here long. I plan on working my way up, you see. One day, I will provide Father with a proper home, because after all the many sacrifices he has made for me over his lifetime, that is what he deserves.

I do not know if I will ever return to America. It was once my home, but I feel adrift. Apart from taking care of Father and spending my days at the bank, I do not know what else is planned for me.

I do not know why I have written you this letter or if you will even reply. You may tear it up and burn it if you so desire. I will not take offense. Honestly, I have no plans of ever hearing from you again, because I understand what is meant for a woman like you and a man like me.

All I want to say is that I am sorry for the pain I caused you. You are a part of my life that I did not plan and I think of our time together on the island often.

If you are ever in London

If you would like to

I wish you the best, dear Louisa. And I hope you find happiness one day, even if it is not with me.

Frederic

Louisa covered her mouth and cried at the realization that Frederic saw no future where they could ever be together. Her tears dripped against the letter until black ink ran down the page. Utterly humiliated, she ripped it up into pieces and opened her window. She paused for a moment and tried to understand the permanence of what she was about to do. There was no guarantee that she would ever receive a letter from Frederic again. Regardless, she gathered up her courage and tossed the remains out the window.

Sinking down to the floor, Louisa listened to the sound of a bird singing outside and buried her face in her hands. How could he expect her to reply back to a letter where he had basically said that they could never be together? Her heart was breaking all over again.

To be considerate, Louisa put on a brave face at dinner that evening, as well as the one after that. Henry and Elaine were so overjoyed with the birth of little Philip, that she felt it would be nothing but selfish to interrupt their joy with her sorrow. So Louisa kept the pain, the heartache, and the letter to herself. Because that was best for everyone else.

Chapter 24

When fall arrived, Louisa sat at the desk by her bedroom window and stared through the glass. With her eighteenth birthday approaching at the end of the year, she felt lost and alone. Her tutoring lessons were done for the day, and the last thing she desired was to look at another history book. Perhaps she should take up a hobby. Learning the craft of a musical instrument would surely distract her from the opened wound inside her heart.

A knock sounded on the door, but Louisa kept her eyes on the outdoors. "You may come in," she called. There was a baby blue robin perched on the tree outside her window. She smiled at the little bird, her thoughts quietly returning to all the many creatures she had encountered in the jungle and might never encounter again.

"Hello, dear," Elaine chimed. With two children under the age of two, she hardly slept at all anymore. In addition, she ran the family business alongside Henry, now that the clothing factory had been restored and in full force over the past year.

Louisa turned to her with a smile and wished that she could glean the satisfaction from life that Elaine seemed to have absorbed so readily. She was thankful to have Elaine as a sister and friend, but longed to have a similar lifestyle for herself. Looking back, she had imagined marriage and children. Only, all of those dreams had been tied to Frederic.

"How are you this afternoon?" Elaine walked into the room and leaned against one of the wooden posts at the end of Louisa's bed. "Did you enjoy your lessons?"

"Yes," Louisa uttered, even though she had not.

Considering her situation, Elaine had done everything in her power to ensure that Louisa would have a proper education from the finest private tutor in New York City. While her time on the island had molded her into the independent woman she was today, Elaine knew all that she had missed in her youth that Louisa would not be deprived of. She wanted to prepare her for the best life possible in America, because that is what Mr. and Mrs. Rochester would have wanted.

"Henry has been called to London for business. The trip should last no more than a week. We were wondering if perhaps you might like to join us," Elaine said.

"Really?" Louisa furrowed her brow. "But what about my studies?"

"I have already spoken with your tutor, and she agreed that you deserve a week off." Elaine approached the desk and patted Louisa on the shoulder. "You have been working so hard. She told me that you are ahead on all of your assignments."

Louisa gazed at the smooth wooden surface of her desk. "It puts my mind at ease."

Elaine set her hands on her hips and nodded, quirking her mouth to the side.

Try as she might, Louisa had failed to move Frederic to the farthest corner of her mind. When she lay down to rest every night, his was the first face to come to mind. She saw his gray eyes and his calm smile. It was a troubling nightmare that kept her awake more evenings than not.

"I'll go," Louisa agreed. She looked up at Elaine and forced a smile.

"Wonderful!" Elaine braided her fingers together, reading the sadness behind Louisa's blue eyes. "Henry will be delighted. We will be taking the children with us as well."

Louisa's face brightened at the sound of her words. They would serve as a lovely distraction to keep her from thinking of Frederic. While in London, it would be hard enough to restrain herself from searching for him night and day.

"Well, I'll leave you to pack. We are leaving in the morning at daybreak."

Nodding at Elaine, Louisa remained still in the chair and watched her sister-in-law leave the room. She never told her about the letter Frederic had sent, even though Elaine would have been the perfect female companion to confide in. Perhaps Louisa knew that she had made a mistake in ripping his words to shreds. But what did it matter now?

Deep down, she longed to run into Frederic while they were in London. The possibility of such a chance encounter made her tremble on the inside. How painful to travel across the pond and not even have a glimpse at him? But she would make the best of the trip and enjoy time spent with her niece and nephew. At least she could breathe the same air as her beloved, and imagine the life that they could have shared together.

Exhaling aloud, Louisa rose to her feet and trudged over to her closet to begin packing. After tossing a few gowns across her mattress, Louisa knelt down on the floor to retrieve the trunk from under her bed. While reaching beneath her bed, she discovered a square piece of paper on the floor. Curious, Louisa leaned in and picked it up.

When she rose from the floor, there was an envelope in her hand with Mr. Frederic Holmes written on the back of it. She stared at his name in black ink for a very long time, recalling that he had been the one to put pen to paper. Following her intuition, Louisa set the envelope down in the trunk and then began packing clothes on top of it.

* * *

Henry waltzed into the hotel suite and drew the curtains back. The streets of London were lively and bustling beneath him, a lovely autumn breeze drifting through the air. "Well, ladies," he crooned, turning back. "What do you make of the place?"

Elaine walked in with Philip in her arms, gently swaying him as he slept. Just as curious, Louisa peered through and stepped inside, little Lilly tugging at her dress. Smiling down at her niece, Louisa picked the child up in her arms and listened to her babbling.

Turning about the large master suite, Elaine gauged the high ceilings and exquisite furniture. While she and Henry had never taken a honeymoon, these accommodations could surely make up for it. She looked over at him with the thought and he winked.

"I love it, Mr. Rochester." Elaine glided over to him and he wrapped his arm around her.

"Truly?" he wondered, eyeing her with intrigue and desire.

"Truly," she echoed, adjusting his collar as she placed a kiss on his cheek.

Little Philip woke with a cry, and Henry reached out to take him. "There now, son." Elaine gently handed Philip over for Henry to hold in his arms. "We have just arrived, and you are already making a fuss." He patted the little boy's back and jostled him in place.

With Elaine's hands free, Lilly reached out to her and squirmed. Louisa set the little girl down as she rushed to her mother, and Elaine picked her up in her arms.

"Well, Louisa," Henry called across the way. "What do you think?"

"Oh, Louisa. I'm sorry." Elaine walked around the bed and pointed to a set of French doors. "Your room is this way. We thought you might like your own space with the children and everything. You know how they can be at night."

Louisa sagged her shoulders in disappointment, because she rather enjoyed comforting the children when they cried at night. Now she would feel even more alone in London.

"Thank you." She left them in the master bedroom and opened the French doors that led to hers. Glancing about the room, she admired the open space and bay windows.

At the sound of pattering footsteps, she turned to see that Lilly had followed her. Delighted at the sight of her niece, Louisa opened her arms and smiled. Lilly giggled and chased after her aunt, practically climbing up her leg so Louisa could carry her.

"Well, what do you think?" Elaine wondered, gazing about the guest room.

"It's lovely, Elaine. Thank you for inviting me along."

"Of course." Elaine glided into the room and turned in a circle to admire it. Then she patted

Louisa on the shoulder and pinched Lilly's cheek until she giggled. "You're family."

Louisa glowed with warmth and smiled. Without Mother and Father, life had never been the same, certain pieces always missing. Separation from Frederic had only deepened the wounds, but now Louisa felt as though she could truly overcome the hurt.

* * *

Tilting her head back, Louisa glanced up and took in the sight of Westminster Bank. Blood thrummed loudly in her ears at the memory of Frederic and all the things he had mentioned in his letter. Including the job he had found at a bank in London.

"Are you ready, ladies?" Henry stood behind her and Elaine, a hand at each of their backs, nudging them along with Lilly and Philip in tow.

"Why must we go in there?" Louisa stared at the tall structure in horror.

"Because I have been called here on business, dear sister." Henry moved past her and opened the door when she hesitated. "It appears we have a new investor."

Louisa went on ahead and then Henry eyed her with a questionable gaze. Even though her heart was nestled at the bottom of her throat, Louisa fought the urge to run away then walked inside. Gazing up at the high ceilings, she felt a chill crawl up her spine at the sight of cool marble.

"Will you watch the children, Louisa?" Henry led the group towards a bench along the far right wall. "Elaine and I will just be a moment."

Louisa nearly panicked, surprised that Elaine would be abandoning her as well. "Sure."

When Louisa took a seat, Lilly pitched a fit and began tugging at her mother's dress. Eventually, Elaine picked her up in her arms and the little girl stopped crying. "Well, what do you know with this one? Perhaps she should come with us, Henry. If I leave her with Louisa, she will carry on for no telling how long and cause a scene."

Henry exhaled and stuffed his hands in his pockets. "You are right, my love."

"I will be fine here, Henry. Just go on. I'll wait here with Philip."

"Good." Henry gestured from one lady to the next. "Shall we?"

Elaine nodded and turned to leave with Henry. They approached a bank teller and chatted away, the man smiling and waving at Lilly until she laughed. Louisa grinned at the sight from afar, happy to be amused, until the teller led them behind the counter and they all disappeared.

Staring down at the baby in her arms, Louisa watched him flutter his long black lashes and glance up at her. Worried that he may cry for his mother, Louisa held her breath until Philip pressed his lips together and sighed. She thought of her mother and father, how thrilled they would have been to witness the birth of another grandchild so soon. But sadly that day would never come. Louisa cradled baby Philip in her arms and whispered sweet promises to him of the beautiful life he was going to have as a Rochester in New York.

Back from a lunch break, Frederic Holmes returned to his post at the bank and placed the CLOSED sign beneath the counter. As he looked across the way for whoever may be next in line, something caught the corner of his eye. Stopping in his tracks, Frederic felt his heart race at the sight of a beautiful blonde sitting on a bench in the distance.

Frederic blinked his eyes several times and wondered if he had lost his mind. But when she laughed, he knew there was no mistaking what he saw. "Louisa," he gasped.

"Excuse me, sir." A woman stood across the counter with an impatient look on her face. "I would like to make a deposit." Helplessly distracted, Frederic had yet to hear her speak, his eyes on the girl on the bench. "Sir," the woman repeated, clearing her throat.

Returning his attention to work, Frederic did as the woman asked and then breathed a sigh of relief when she was gone. Since no one else had approached, Frederic set his sights on Louisa and came out from behind the counter. When he noticed the newborn in her arms, his heart dropped. All this time, he had been trying to create a better life for himself, a life that Louisa would approve of, a life that she might even like to share. But now it was clear to see that he was too late.

Just as he turned to walk away, the voice of an angel murmured, "Frederic?"

Paralyzed by the sound, Frederic turned back around and came closer than he had before. Close enough to truly see Louisa and drink her in. Blonde hair. Blue eyes. Ivory skin and all. Nearly a year had passed, yet she hadn't aged a day. Still young and beautiful.

"Ms. Rochester," he greeted. "What a wonderful surprise."

"Hello, Frederic." Her mouth went dry and her heart was about to burst, but in that moment she was truly content. Her wish to see Frederic one last time had come true.

"Well, I will leave you to look after your son." Frederic curved his lips upward into a smile that flashed across his face like a bolt of lightning. Gone just before the thunder.

"Frederic, wait." Louisa stood with Philip in her arms and compelled Frederic to turn back around for the second time. "He is not my son."

Confused, Frederic glanced down at the baby and then back to her honest eyes, true blue as the sky. For a moment, he believed that her mission was to spare his feelings, but Louisa had never been a liar. Then he noted her bare left hand. A ring was missing.

"Oh," was all Frederic could muster.

"Meet my nephew, Philip Rochester. My brother's son," she explained.

Struck with realization, Frederic stared at the child with a sense of understanding.

"Henry and Elaine," Louisa went on. "They also have a daughter, named Lilly."

Feeling as though he were walking in a daydream, Frederic looked over Louisa and smiled. He longed to reach out and touch her but caught himself and resisted.

"How are you, Frederic?" Louisa peered into his silvery eyes like she was looking through a glass pane, desperate to see what was on the other side.

"All right, I suppose." He chewed at his bottom lip and could not seem to take his eyes off her.

"I wonder," he mused, leaning in closer. "Did you ever receive my letter?"

Louisa looked down and held Philip to her breast. "Yes," she whispered. "I did."

"Oh," Frederic nodded. Chills shot through his veins at her reaction. He felt as though he were moments away from melting and would have no way of standing up again.

When the baby squeezed his tiny hands together and cried, Louisa stroked his cheek with the end of her finger. Frederic lowered his eyes to admire her display of tender affection. He had never wanted to make one of his own with her so badly.

"What brings you to London?" Frederic asked, merely to make the conversation last a moment more. He would have given anything to spend the rest of his day in her company.

"Family business," she answered. "Henry and Elaine are in the back sorting out some matter with one of your colleagues." She nodded her head past the counter.

"If I had known, Louisa." Without thinking, he inched closer and touched her elbow. "I would have helped you all the moment you arrived."

Louisa gave him a shy smile, as only Louisa could. "That is quite all right."

When her eyes darted to the counter, Frederic looked back over his shoulder at his supervisor. He should have thought twice before rushing to Louisa. It hardly looked favorable that he had abandoned the counter during his shift.

"I must go," he sadly stated. "But I would like to see you again before you leave." Anxious to feel her warmth, he rested his palms on her shoulders. "How long will you be in London?"

"We leave on Sunday." Louisa lifted her head and gazed deeply into his eyes.

"Sunday," he repeated, nodding his head ever so slightly. "May I see you tomorrow?"

"Yes," she sweetly replied. Her blue eyes shined and were burning bright.

"Wonderful." He traced his thumb along her cheek and then set his finger beneath her chin. "I must go now," he crooned in reluctance. "I will see you tomorrow."

"All right." She tingled at the intimacy of his touch.

"Until tomorrow then." Frederic smirked at the fresh blush against her cheeks. Then he cast his eyes on the baby and added, "Please tell your brother and his wife that I said hello."

"I will," Louisa chimed, already missing his hand on her face. "I will."

"I'm glad." With a mournful sigh, Frederic turned on his heel and returned to his place behind the counter. All the while, he felt as though someone were staring at him. When he resumed his post, a lingering smile fell across his face. Because the eyes of his admirer were an innocent, soft, endearing shade of blue.

Chapter 25

Goodbye, my love." Henry kissed Elaine and headed for the door. "I will be back in an hour."

"All right." Elaine rolled over in bed, stretching out like a lazy house cat. She turned onto her side and reached for her robe, slipping into the smooth satin as she prepared for her day. The moment Henry left, the room filled with silence.

When there was a knock at the door, Elaine hurried to a mirror to ensure that her hair was tame enough to be seen. She assumed that Louisa was still asleep in the guest room and could hardly believe that today was their last in London. The trip had been a lovely departure from New York, but Elaine truly was ready to be home.

By the time Elaine opened the door, whoever had rapped against the frame was gone. She would have voiced a concern if not for the cart covered with trays of hot, delicious food waiting for them. Shrugging it off, Elaine steered the breakfast cart into the master suite and elevated the heel of her foot to shut the door behind her.

Once she sat down, Elaine fixed herself a plate and buttered the first blueberry muffin she saw. Almost immediately, Louisa came in from the guest room and ambled over to the table. She threaded her fingers through her blonde locks and took a seat beside Elaine.

"Good morning, Louisa. Would you like some breakfast?"

"Yes," Louisa replied. She watched Elaine fix two cups of tea and sighed. "I am expecting a visitor today," she confessed.

"Really?" Elaine stabbed an egg with her fork. "Who?"

"Frederic." Louisa flushed red at the mention of his name. "We spoke yesterday at the bank."

"Yes," Elaine admitted. "Henry and I saw Mr. Holmes yesterday as well, only we were not sure whether or not we should mention it to you. What did he have to say?"

"We only spoke for a moment, because he had to return to work."

Elaine reached for the jar of jam and spotted a white card beneath it. Curious as ever, she set the jar down and unfolded the card. There was an address inside written in an elegant hand with black ink. A ruby red feather slipped out and fell in her lap.

"I suppose it will be nice to see Frederic today," Louisa mused. "I have missed him." She pressed her cheek against her palm and looked off in a state of melancholy.

"Will you be all right to look after the children for a while?" Elaine asked.

Louisa furrowed her brow as Elaine stood up and hurried about to get dressed. "Yes. Why? Where are you going? You have hardly even touched your breakfast."

Elaine slipped into an elegant emerald gown and ran a comb through her hair.

"Are you leaving?" Louisa turned back in her seat with a frown.

"Yes, Louisa." She stepped into a pair of shoes and adjusted the straps. Before long, her hair and makeup were immaculate as she spritzed on a dab of sweet smelling perfume.

"But, Elaine." Louisa chased after Elaine when she practically sprinted out the door. "I don't understand. Where are you going? Why are you off in such a hurry?"

Elaine pressed her lips into a flat line and patted Louisa on the shoulder. "There is somewhere that I need to be. I will not be gone long. Look over Lilly and Philip."

Utterly perplexed, Louisa stood alone in the master suite as Elaine shut the door behind her as if the whole world were about to come crashing down. When Lilly toddled into the room and extended her hands with a cry, Louisa picked the little girl up in her arms and held her tight. For a moment, she recalled that Frederic was on his way and nearly panicked. She hoped that he liked children.

* * *

Elaine stood before the taxidermist's office with a look of misunderstanding on her face. The card read 234 Willow Street but she was standing in front of 235 Willow Street, and the closest building was named 233 Willow Street. Just as she turned to flee, a teenage boy with shaggy dark hair and deep brown eyes opened the door.

"Hello, I am looking for..." She gazed down at the card again to be sure. "234 Willow Street?"

"Hello, Ms. Carmichael," he muttered, opening the door. "Right this way."

A thrill of fear rippled through her, but she could not deny the urge to see what was inside. "All right." She grabbed the skirt of her gown and stepped inside. "Thank you."

The young lad pulled the door closed behind them and disappeared into the back. As mesmerized as she was horrified by her surroundings, Elaine scanned the room full of stuffed creatures. Wild deer, grizzly bears, foxes—red and gray. She felt as though she were being watched by the eyes of the many still animals.

After regarding every creature, Elaine lingered towards the back of the shop at the sight of two big cats. Her heart fluttered against her chest once the mother leopard and black panther came into view. It was rather odd, that she had been a witness to their killing over a year ago and now they were here, stuffed in a London shop on display for all to see.

"Fancy anything in particular?"

Elaine stiffened at the sound of boots across the ground. Feeling the warmth of his body behind her, Elaine turned around and gazed into a pair of dark eyes. "Hello."

Captain Scarlett smiled and looked over her figure with desire. "Motherhood becomes you, Mrs. Rochester." He took her hand and kissed the back of it.

"Gregory," Elaine inhaled, removing her hand from his grasp.

He nodded once in understanding and slid to the side, extending his arm out for her to follow his lead. Feeling on edge, Elaine followed Captain Scarlett through the shop and down a long dark corridor. When they reached the door at the end of the hall, Captain Scarlett opened it, so Elaine gingerly entered the room and took a seat inside.

"Your office, I presume?" Elaine set her glistening green eyes on him.

"Yes, Mrs. Rochester." He swept his long fingers through his smooth dark locks and sat down on the other side of his desk. "My office."

"Why have you called me here today, Gregory?" Elaine felt unease at the thought that tracking her down had posed no problem. Who had been watching her?

"Once on the island, you told me that you

could not understand how Judas was alive. You plunged a dagger into his heart, and yet there he was again. Do you remember?"

Elaine looked down and clutched the card with the address on it in her lap. "Yes," she blubbered. "Yes, I remember."

"Judas sometimes wore this beneath his shirt." Captain Scarlett tossed a stuffed bag onto his desk. "It is filled with broken wood and the blood of animals."

Elaine quirked her brow at him in disbelief.

"The wood creates a weapon, an illusion of a musculature torso. When you stabbed him in the heart, it punched through the bag instead. But you saw blood and believed what you wanted to believe."

Elaine shook her head. "This doesn't make any sense. I don't understand."

"I am in the process of developing a line for soldiers. A protective vest if you will. In time, my knowledge and skill set will improve. Perhaps one day it will repel bullets."

"Why do you care to tell me exactly how Judas survived?"

Captain Scarlett walked around the desk and leaned against the edge of it. When he cocked his head to the side and watched Elaine, she pressed her lips together and swallowed. Even without the hat, he sure knew how to cast an intimidating look.

"I just thought you might like to know."

Elaine lowered her lashes and then looked off

to the side, spotting a framed picture on the wall. Thoroughly intrigued, she stood up from the chair and walked over to the photograph. Something about the other man in it looked oddly familiar.

"Gregory?" she chirped. "Who is the man in this photograph standing next to you?"

Gliding towards her, Captain Scarlett slipped an arm across her back and rested his chin over her shoulder. "Oh, merely a distant cousin of mine, Charles Gallagher."

Struck with familiarity, Elaine turned her head to the side as Captain Scarlett leaned in for a kiss. Pushing him away with her hand in his face, Elaine waltzed over to the other side of the room as her mind surged round and round. "Dead or alive?"

"Young Charles is deceased, unfortunately," Captain Scarlett revealed.

Elaine narrowed her glistening green gaze on him and waited for more.

"I believe it was a shipwreck of some kind out in the Atlantic."

Moistening her lower lip, Elaine took a deep breath and asked, "Who are you?"

With a sly smirk, Captain Scarlett stalked towards Elaine and stopped once his face nearly touched hers. "I am no one, Mrs. Rochester. No one of any importance."

"No." Elaine backed into the wall and pointed a finger at him. "You saw something. You know something. What is it? What are you hiding?"

Captain Scarlett placed his hands on the wall

behind Elaine and caged her body in with his arms. "I know secrets that would keep you up at night for years. I know things. Things that no one should ever know. I am cursed, you see. For life. For death."

"What does that mean?" Elaine hissed, feeling his warm breath on her cheek.

Captain Scarlett covered her mouth with a kiss to silence her, but Elaine slapped him across the face as soon as he let her pull away. "My, you do enjoy striking me."

"What is your name?" She paced the floor until she reached the opposite wall. "Your real name?"

Captain Scarlett sank his teeth into his lower lip and rocked back on his heels. Then he crossed his arms over his chest and said, "I've already told you my real name."

"You are no more Gregory Scarlett than Judas was William Pierce."

"Gregory is my real name," he insisted. "I did not lie to you."

Elaine narrowed her eyes and scowled until he inevitably gave in.

"Gregory Winchester," he finally declared. "Happy?"

"Not in the slightest." Elaine judged him with her chin in the air.

Rolling his eyes, Captain Scarlett retreated to the liquor cabinet in the back of the room where he poured himself a glass of gin. After downing the drink in one swallow, he opened the closet and pulled out a black fur coat. Elaine watched him with dissatisfaction and hoped that she had failed to interpret the situation for what it was.

"For you, my lady." Captain Scarlett tossed the coat in the air, and she caught it.

"What is this?" She clutched the mass of fur in her palms and dug her nails in.

"Your jungle cat," he explained. "All that is left of her."

Elaine glanced down at the glossy black pelt, and her hands turned limp. As tears came to her eyes, she glowered at Captain Scarlett and tossed the coat on the ground. Then she marched towards him raging with hatred and beat her fists against his breast.

"How could you? You know what she meant to me! How could you?" she cried.

Captain Scarlett grabbed her wrists and pinned them to her sides. When Elaine continued thrashing and flailing about, he took her face in his hands and kissed her. Even though she tried to fight him off, Captain Scarlett pressed her back into the wall and molded his mouth to hers. By the time he came up for air, she was gritting her teeth.

"I would apologize for that, but it would be a lie." Captain Scarlett picked up the bottle of gin and took a large gulp. "I am leaving London. After tonight, you will never have to look at me again."

Elaine wiped the back of her hand against her

mouth, scrubbing his taste away.

"Take the coat, Elaine. Not for prancing about at the theatre." He turned back and looked directly into her piercing glare. "Take it to remember her by."

Still shaking with outrage, Elaine bent down and swiped the fur coat off the floor. "I'm not sure why I even came," she spat at him. "What a foolish choice to see you."

"Of course you came," Captain Scarlett uttered in a voice that was velvety smooth. "You were curious." Clenching her jaw, Elaine turned on her heel and ran into the hall.

He heard her shoes clacking against the cold hard ground until she barged out of the shop and slammed the door behind her. Drowning in misery, he refilled his glass with gin and sucked it down. When it was empty, he threw the glass across the room and it collided with the wall and shattered into a hundred tiny pieces.

Sinking to the floor, Captain Scarlett inhaled at the pain and drank gin from the bottle. By tomorrow, her tropical scent would be gone, just like his chance of ever seeing her again. Forever. So he hung his head and tore his fingers through his hair.

Even pirates cry.

Chapter 26

Louisa nearly bit her fingernails off while she paced back and forth in the hotel suite. Lilly and Philip sat on the bed looking left to right as she marched from one side of the room to the other. Exceptionally nervous, she twirled her finger through a long blonde lock of hair and tugged.

"What will he say?" Louisa wondered. "What will he do? How do I look?"

She stopped pacing and turned to Lilly and Philip in her sapphire blue gown.

But then there was a knock at the door, and her heart nearly soared out of her chest. Widening her blue eyes in fear, Louisa smoothed out the folds of her dress and glanced at her niece and nephew one last time. Philip had fallen asleep and Lilly sat there with her head cocked to the side. Surely, they both thought Aunt Louisa had gone mad.

Louisa shut her eyes, took a deep breath, and

put one foot in front of the other. When she opened the door, Frederic looked dapper standing on the other side of it. Elated to see him, she took a step back and widened the gap in the door. "Please, come in."

Frederic stepped into the hotel room and immediately spotted the two little ones on the bed. "Well, hello there!" He carefully approached and sat down beside Lilly.

Delighted at his immediate reaction, Louisa shut the door and sauntered towards the bed.

"What is your name?" he wondered, wagging a finger at Lilly.

Frightened by the new stranger, Lilly turned her back and ran into Louisa's arms. "Aww..." Louisa pulled her into her embrace and cuddled her close. "Don't be frightened, darling. It is just Frederic here to see your Aunt Louisa."

Regardless, Lilly placed her head on Louisa's shoulder and looked away.

"Ah! There is the other one," Frederic joked, pointing to Philip snoozing on the bed.

"Yes, I believe you and Philip have already been acquainted," Louisa chimed.

Frederic kept his eyes on her face as he said, "It is awfully good to see you."

Louisa blushed and lowered her gaze, suddenly recalling the harsh separation they had endured. His words from that cold December night came rushing back to her and she shivered.

"Why have you come, Frederic?" Louisa

began. Before he could reply, she sailed into a set of questions. "Why did you send that letter? After all this time, what more could you possibly have to say?"

Frederic inhaled and parted his lips with a breath. "I know that I have hurt you."

Louisa ignored him and rubbed Lilly's back, the pain setting in full force.

"But I must know how you have been."

Aiming to distract herself, Louisa placed Philip in his bassinette and then Lilly in her crib. With her hands free, it would be easier to fend him off should she need to. He must understand the great magnitude with which he had destroyed her, an aching, bruising, bottomless pit of agony that would never implode or converge. It would never heal.

Frederic stepped down from the bed and walked up behind Louisa. She pulled the gossamer curtains back and gazed down at the bustling city streets below. "Do you like it here in London, Frederic?" she wondered.

"I am rather indifferent to the place," he admitted, surprising her.

"Why?" She clung to the curtain with all of her strength. It was her only form of support.

"Because there is no seeing you."

Louisa shut her eyes as a lonesome teardrop slipped through. How could he come here and speak of such things to her? Was his only purpose to be her eternal torment?

"Well, I thought that was the way you wanted it, Frederic." She turned to flee, but he grabbed her arm so there was no chance of escape. "What do you want?"

"Louisa. Please." He gazed longingly into her eyes. "I have something to say."

"Well then, say it!" she snapped, hating the way he tugged at her emotions so.

Frederic silenced her with a kiss and cradled her face in his hands. When she sighed at the tingling sensation, he watched her dark lashes flutter and rubbed his thumb along her jawline. But then she regained consciousness and slammed her eyes wide open.

"What was that?" she declared. "You have nothing to say?"

"Louisa, darling," he chuckled. "Believe me. That kiss said everything."

She bit her lip to keep from laughing, as warm blood rushed to her cheeks. When he leaned in for another kiss, she swayed backward but he met her halfway and brought her mouth to his. By the time she grew dizzy, Louisa clung to his strong arms for support.

"I have just received a promotion to a bank in New York," he rasped.

"Really?" Louisa saw the fire in his eyes. "When?"

"Last week," he answered. "Father and I are leaving London at the end of the month."

Trembling with excitement, Louisa planted her

hand on his chest and opened her mouth in awe. "Frederic, I—"

Ravenous with desire, he pushed her body up against the wall and breathed across her face. Louisa stared at him and swallowed, gasping for air. When he saw the love and affection for him in her eyes, Frederic tenderly cupped her cheek in his palm.

"I want you to be my wife," he professed.

"What?" She could hardly get the word out, in too much of a state of shock.

"Will you be my wife?" he asked, tracing his fingertips over her cheek.

"Frederic. Frederic, I—"

"Don't leave me hanging out here to dry, Louisa. I need your answer."

Speechless and hardly able to breathe, she rested her forehead against his and whispered, "Yes."

Biting his lower lip, Frederic leaned into the warmth of her body and covered her mouth with his kiss. When she whimpered, he pulled back and looked her over.

"I haven't even bought you a ring yet," he realized, embarrassed.

"I don't care." She fell into his embrace and wrapped her arms around him.

Frederic grinned and squeezed her tight, cherishing her lips with kiss after kiss.

"I must go," he finally said. "I don't trust myself around you, sweet Louisa."

Glowing with warmth, she leaned up on the tips of her toes and clung to his side while he dragged himself to the door. Once he reached it, Frederic grabbed the handle and forced himself into the hall. Louisa lingered in the doorway and shot him a wink.

"We will meet again soon, my love." He planted a gentle kiss on the back of her hand.

"When are you going to start calling me Mrs. Holmes?" she teased.

"Sooner than you think." He crushed his lips to hers and then skipped down the hall without looking back.

Swelling with satisfaction, Louisa watched him until he faded away. When she shut the door and waltzed back into the hotel suite, her body gave way and she collapsed on the mattress, utterly glowing. At the sound of Lilly's cry, Louisa rushed over to her niece and picked her up in her arms.

"Oh, come now baby girl. Don't cry. Your Aunt Louisa is getting married."

Rocking the child back and forth, Louisa beamed from cheek to cheek, her heart about to burst with excitement. Somehow, her wish had come true. Frederic had returned to her arms, where he had always belonged, and he was irrevocably hers.

Chapter 27

Elaine exhaled in irritation at the realization of being called to the factory on a Sunday afternoon. But her husband had asked for her help, and she was willing to give it.

When she arrived, Elaine strolled through the open factory until she saw the glass window with her last name scripted across the front. Clutching the skirt of her dress, Elaine climbed the steps until she reached the top. Henry was waiting for her in the office. Alone.

"What is it, darling?" She rushed forward and stilled at the sight of a package.

Henry sat down on the edge of his desk and eyed it carefully.

"What is that?" Elaine felt her heart throbbing against her ribcage.

Tired of waiting, Henry opened his pocket knife and cut into the box. Elaine turned in the other direction and pushed the heel of her hand against her forehead. She could not cope with the potential outcome. The last time they had received a mysterious package, danger had been entirely too close.

Henry ripped through the top of the box and tossed the knife to his desk. Breath caught at the back of his throat, while his eyes widened in astonishment. "Elaine."

With a deep breath, she looked over her shoulder and prepared herself for whatever lay inside the box. One step and then another, until Elaine was face to face with her prize. For dramatic effect, Henry ripped the flap down and gold coins spilled out and scattered across the floor.

Diamonds. Emeralds. Rubies. Pearls. Sapphires. Silver. Gold.

Every bit of treasure from the island from every crevice where it had remained hidden. Elaine shook her head in shock, hardly able to believe that it could be true. Beaming with joy, Henry sifted his hands through the jewels and laughed at the absurdity of it.

"Henry, is that... How?" Her finger remained pointed in the air.

Thrilled at the prospect of never-ending financial freedom, Henry pulled Elaine close and kissed her on the mouth. Then he pushed her hair over her shoulder and wrapped an arm around her. Strangely, she had yet to warm to the hidden treasure.

"Who sent it?" she wondered, curiosity eating

at her.

"Our new investor." Henry handed her a white card. "The one who wished to remain anonymous," he reminded her from their trip to the bank.

Elaine flipped the card over and found the word Winchester embossed in black.

"Winchester," Henry read. "I'm afraid I don't recognize that name. Do you know it?"

"No." Elaine shook her head in still silence.

Noticing a crease in the card, Elaine furrowed her brow and opened the fold.

A ruby red feather slipped out and floated to the ground.

Tell Me Your Favorite Part!

If you enjoyed Coastal Spirit, I invite you to head over to Amazon and let me know your favorite part. Reviews are so important to an author's career, because they help new readers like you discover the book. Even if you didn't enjoy Coastal Spirit, I'd still love it if you could take three minutes to let me know what you think of the book.

Leaving a review is super easy:

1) Go to Coastal Spirit Book Page on Amazon

2) Scroll Down and click "Write a Customer Review"

3) Sign in to Amazon if prompted

4) Select a star rating

5) Write a few short words (or long words, I won't judge)

6) Click the 'submit' button

I thank you in advance!

Acknowledgements

First of all, I would like to thank my awesome, amazing parents for believing in my dreams from the very start. You guys read my stories back in high school when I never imagined they would materialize into much. Thank you for cheering me on at every turn. You'll always be remembered as my original fans. Back when Tom and Addie were no more than a secret kept between the three of us.

Special thanks to my extended family and friends for the much needed breaks from my crazy writing schedule. Sometimes all I need is some popcorn and a movie. I can't think of anyone else I would rather break bread with after a long day. Y'all keep me sane ;)

Thank you to Kylie, George, and Jeananna at Give Me Books. You lessen the stress of Release Week and spread the word to those who don't even know my name. To all the bloggers/reviewers who sign up for every event, you guys rock! I would never be able to get through Cover Reveals & Release Blitzes without every single one of you. So thank you!

Susan Meachen at Authors & Readers Café: You have absolutely rocked my world with your love for *An Arrangement*. I cannot thank you enough for spreading the word about Benny and Claire. I never imagined so many people would have that story in their hands, and I am overwhelmed with the positive feedback it has received. Thank You <3

Rose & Margie at Can't Stop Reading Blog: Thank you for letting me do my first ever Author Takeover with you lovely ladies! I appreciate your support in helping me spread the word with upcoming releases. Rock On! :)

I would also like to thank SJ's Book Blog, Kylie's Fiction Addiction, Reading Between the Wines Book Club, The Howling Turtle, Sassy Book Lovers, More than Scribbles, Celtic Lady's Reviews, Lisa Loves Literature, Nerd Girl, Love Books, Sapphyria's Book Reviews, Word Spelunking, Socrates' Book Review, Paulette's Papers, Mrs. Mommy Booknerd, Rolo Polo Book Blog, Keep Calm and Write On, I Read Indie, A is for Alpha B is for Book, Penny for My Thoughts, Yah Gotta Read This, Amazeballs Book Addicts,

Who Picked This? and any of the other awesome bloggers out there that I might have missed. Y'all are awesome :)

To the lovely authors I have met out there in indie world including Jessica Hernandez, Lauren L. Garcia, Aubrey Parr, Amanda Leigh, India R. Adams, Tee Smith, Micalea Smeltzer, Molly E. Lee and Addison Moore. Every one of you deserves a huge shout-out, and I look forward to watching y'all craft new stories in the years to come.

Last but not least, I would like to thank you, the reader. You are the lifeblood of my journey as an author, and without you I would never have the opportunity to turn my daydreams and fantasies into full-fledged novels. However you came across my name, thank you for reading and experiencing the world of *Coastal Spirit*. I hope Henry and Elaine brought some light into your day and helped you escape to the jungle, even if it was only for a little while. Much love, hugs and kisses to you all... :)

About the Author

Lindsay Marie Miller was born and raised in Tallahassee, Florida, where she graduated from high school as Valedictorian. At sixteen, she started writing her first novel, *Emerald Green*, after being inspired by Stephenie Meyer's International Bestselling *Twilight Saga*. During her time in college, Lindsay wrote 5 more novels and over 100 songs. After graduating Summa Cum Laude from Florida State University, she put her B.A. in English Literature to good use and published her debut novel, *Emerald Green*. An author of over 10 Romance Titles, Lindsay currently resides in her hometown of Tallahassee where she is always working on her next novel.

To learn more, please visit:

www.lindsaymariemillerauthor.com

Sign up for Lindsay's newsletter:

lindsaymariemillerauthor.com/claim-your-free-book/

Join Lindsay on Facebook at:

facebook.com/LindsayMarieMillerAuthor

Follow Lindsay on Twitter at:

twitter.com/Lindsay_MMiller

Here's a sneak peek of

EMERALD GREEN,

an electrifying romantic thriller.

Chapter 1

I stepped out into the cold dark night, searching for a familiar face in the parking lot. With a crumpled fold of white chiffon in my hand, I gently shut the car door, wondering why Eric was nowhere to be found. Locking my silver Volkswagen Beetle with the push of a button, I glided across the black pavement. The incessant clicking of my heels against the ground made me even more aware of my presence in a formal white gown.

The Winter Ball had never been my idea, but Eric had insisted, since his antiquated high school did not host dances. Maple Creek High, on the other hand, had no problem renting a Hilton hotel ballroom for the evening. With the rate of tuition increasing every year, the PTA felt no remorse in demanding what they wanted.

Inside the ballroom, a cluster of students migrated towards the center of the dance floor. Teenage boys jostled into each other, too distracted by the cleavage-baring dresses worn by their teasing girlfriends. Junior quarterback, Ricky Travis, danced at the front of the crowd with his very own Barbie doll, Nicki Caldwell.

Nicki wore an ocean blue dress with aquamarine jewels scattered along the neckline, though she looked more like a mermaid than a princess. Her white blonde curls were stacked atop her head, clasped together with a lavender seashell clip, while a string of pearls clung to either of her small, bony wrists. Even in December, Nicki was ready for the beach.

To achieve her picture-perfect appearance, Nicki frequented salons on a weekly basis, where she allowed beauticians to bleach her hair, burn her skin, and coat her nails with a new shade of candy-colored polish. Once the tanning process was complete, Nicki laid down ample amounts of cold, hard cash, so that a professional could wax the places on her body where she had rather not have hair. And yet, Ricky pressed his body against hers, wrapping his arms around her stomach, as if she had woken up like this.

I could not help but roll my eyes.

Ricky Travis had spent the past two years tugging at my hair in math class. Somehow, every semester, at least one teacher's seating chart always indicated that Ricky would be sitting in the seat directly behind mine. If I ever turned around, Ricky would let go of my hair, holding his hands in the air as if he were an innocent man. "I didn't do anything," he would smugly remark, his thin lips held apart.

The truth is, I had developed a crush on Ricky at the start of freshman year, when we all began taking classes at Maple Creek High. He was tall, dark, handsome, and athletic. But it only took two weeks for me to discover his wicked ways.

I sauntered around the edge of the dance floor and removed the cream-colored coat from my shoulders. No one stood at the punch table, so I poured myself a drink. The cherry flavored liquid felt pungent on my tongue, as I shriveled my face in disgust. When I looked up, a young girl approached, who could have been no older than fifteen.

"Ricky poisoned it," the girl said. Her black bob slightly bounced as she spoke.

"What?" I set the plastic cup down on the table, carefully looking her over.

"I mean with alcohol." She shrugged her shoulders, then turned towards the dance floor to look at Ricky. "He's my brother."

"Oh." I raised my eyebrows, then placed a hand at my waist. "My condolences."

The girl laughed at my snide remark, drawing attention to her doll-like figure. "I'm Jeanine." She stuck her small hand forward, shaking mine. "And you're Addie Smith."

"Yes." I nodded. "How do you know my name?"

"Ricky." She pointed over her shoulder, while

her older brother gyrated against Nicki's tight-skirted bottom. "He talks about you all the time."

"Really?" I caught Ricky's eye across the dance floor. He froze in place, then passed Nicki off to another football player, as the next techno-pop song began.

"I better go." Jeanine grew stoic and frightened. Her red lips looked as though they were quivering. "Don't tell him what I told you."

"All right." I watched her scamper away, not understanding our brief, yet telling conversation. When Ricky approached, I turned my back to him, studying the punch bowl before me.

"Hello Addie," Ricky murmured. I could feel his breath at the back of my neck.

I turned to face him. "What do you want?" I pressed my palm into his chest, pushing him away. Ricky leaned against the punch table, reclining on his elbows.

"Just to tell you how beautiful you look tonight." Ricky pulled at my hair. I slapped his hand away, sighing in frustration. Nicki walked up to me, the hatred evident in her eyes.

I looked at Ricky, then grabbed the folds of my white gown. "You're ridiculous." I stormed off, in search of the bathroom, leaving Nicki to contemplate the behavior of her boyfriend.

On my way down a long corridor, I heard the sound of someone crying. Jeanine sat in the hallway, with her back against the wall. Her bright red party dress fell in ruffled folds, just above the knee.

"Jeanine, what's wrong?" I knelt down beside her, not minding that I might stain my white dress.

"Can you drive me home? Please! I don't want to go home with Ricky." Heavy tears streamed down her face, pulling streaks of black mascara with them.

"All right," I succumbed, resting my hand on her shoulder. "You're a freshman aren't you?"

"Yes." She nodded.

"And we had a class together?" I squinted my eyes in a questioning manner.

"Study hall," she whimpered, unable to look me in the eye.

I took a deep breath, blowing hot air through my teeth. "Wait here, I'll find the back door to this place." I rose, slipping back into my winter coat.

"Addie, thank you," she whispered, choking on her own tears. "And I'm sorry I ruined your night."

"It's all right, honey. My date didn't show anyway." I patted her on the shoulder before walking off.

I turned at the end of the hallway, noticing a red EXIT sign above a door. I pushed the door open and climbed three flights of stairs, before reaching an old wooden door at the top. Turning the tarnished metal knob, I crossed the threshold and found a dark, empty room.

"Hello," I called out, stepping forward. But as

I let go of the heavy door, it swung back into the door frame, slamming in place. I twisted the doorknob, frowning at its immobility. The door was locked.

"Hello." I banged my fist against the door, yelling for help. "Jeanine!" But she wasn't going to hear me. I had left her in the hallway three floors below.

After fifteen minutes of hollering, I set my purse down and removed the thick warm coat that hung over my gown. The room smelled of dust and sweat. I wondered why the hotel had yet to remodel it, as renovations had been completed on the rest of the building just before the Winter Ball date had been set.

All was dark in the room, except for a small, square window that revealed a sliver of moonlight, which shone down on the floor below. I stepped into the pale white light and watched the half-moon hang in the black sky. A translucent layer of dense fog surrounded the moon, drawing further attention to its true silvery radiance.

"Addie," a strange voice said. I felt a cool hand touch the bare skin of my shoulder. My heart thumped loudly inside of my chest as I swallowed, too terrified to turn around. Lifting my eyes to the window, I spotted his reflection in the glass. His black, neatly cropped hair looked like Ricky's, though not exactly. Unable to resist my fear any longer, I turned around. The man who stood before me was not Ricky.

"Hello." He smiled, standing much closer than I would have liked. A pair of straight white teeth glimmered in the moonlight as I recoiled, pressing my body into the window. Privy to my fear, he held his hands up in innocence and backed away from me.

Breathing heavily, I closed my eyes, and then opened them again, only to find him staring at the stretch of wall beside me. He kept still, letting his arms hang down at his sides, as I took a step towards him. Once I followed his gaze, I realized that he was not staring at the wall, but at the painting that hung there.

It was a portrait of a young woman, no more than eighteen. She sat still in the moonlight, gently holding her palms together, over her lap. Long thick locks of golden blonde hair framed her face and fell to the middle of her back. The hair was silky, wavy, and looked as though it had been fashioned from an angel's wings.

The woman's frame appeared thin, fragile even, yet her complexion was less fair than one would have imagined, presumably from hours spent beneath the summer sun.

Though of all her soft, gentle features, the most remarkable was the magic, liquid luster of her emerald green eyes. She was beautiful.

"You remind me so much of her," he whispered in the darkness.

A white satin gown was draped over her shoulders, flowing around the rest of her slim body. I looked down at my own dress, unable to deny the similarities. *The hair. The eyes. The skin.* It was all the same. If not for the emerald stone around her neck, I would have thought I was looking in a mirror.

"Who is she?" I extended my hand, moving close enough to touch the portrait. But before my finger could trace the stone, all of it disappeared.

* * *

I woke in the darkness, lying on a bed of white sheets. Recognizing my bedroom, I turned to the lamp on my nightstand and switched it on. The clock by my bed indicated that it was three o'clock in the morning. I pulled the sheet back, sank my feet into the carpet, and lost my balance. Stumbling to the wooden chair near the window, I found my white formal gown and winter coat that lay draped over the seat. For the life of me, I could not remember putting them there.

I thought about the strange dream. The boy seemed familiar to me, somehow. He had jet black hair and a tall, muscular build, like Ricky. Yet, there was something different about the two of them. Both had brown eyes, but they were not quite the same. Ricky's eyes had always been a strange mixture of red and brown, like the color of a maple leaf. But the boy, the stranger, his eyes were golden brown, almost the shade of honey, with flecks of yellow sprinkled throughout.

I spent the next several nights sketching the boy's eyes. I started with a thin gray pencil to outline the shape of them. Then, I filled the pupils with black before coloring the irises with a blend of orange, yellow, and brown. By the time I was finished, the eyes reminded me of autumn, when all the leaves begin to change in color and hue.

I looked out at the tree that stood before my bedroom window. All of the leaves were gone.

Chapter 2

After New Year's, Maple Creek High was back in session. It had been over a week since I had seen Jeanine Travis at the Winter Ball, yet she found me just after the first bell rang. I was carelessly shoving books into my locker, not minding who was standing close enough to notice.

"Hey Addie," Jeanine said. She was wearing a candy apple red headband over her black bob. It rested just behind the line where her bangs began.

"Hi," I replied, smiling at her. I tried to remember if I had driven her home that night, but the last thing I could recall was finding her in the hallway, crying. "Did everything work out all right at the dance?"

"Yeah," she piped up, her voice escalating in pitch. Then, her eyes flicked to the side and she turned her head down. "I'm sorry about my brother," she whispered, discreetly glancing over her shoulder to see if anyone else was listening.

"It's okay." I shut my locker, beaming in her

direction. Jeanine nodded, her voice turning quiet all of a sudden. "Well, don't be late for class." I turned on my heel and waved, as I walked down the hall towards homeroom.

I sat down in the front row, waiting for Mrs. Thompson to hand out our class schedules. I retrieved a sketchbook from my backpack and began drawing on the first page.

"Addie Smith," Mrs. Thompson called. I took the schedule from her, looking down to see what the semester held.

Name: Addie Smith

Year: Junior

Homeroom

1st period: Chemistry

2nd period: British Literature

3rd period: Trigonometry

4th period: Gym

Lunch

5th period: Western Civilization

6th period: Latin

7th period: Psychology

I was happy to see that I no longer had gym

class first period. I curled my lip at chemistry and nearly barked at trigonometry. The curriculum had been tolerable for fall semester, but this spring semester schedule made me cringe.

Maple Creek High was ranked in the top five for college preparatory schools in Georgia. Atlanta always nabbed the top four spots with their top of the line educational facilities. In all honesty, we were lucky that Savannah had even made it on the list, much less received a fifth place standing.

At the sound of the bell, I packed my things and headed upstairs to the chemistry lab. I knew that Mr. Martinez was an easy grader and gave out bonus points for showing up. Nonetheless, I felt a nest of butterflies flutter around in my stomach when I entered the lab. The entrance was at the back of the classroom, with all of the tables and chairs facing the opposite direction, towards the whiteboard.

Each table held two chairs that sat beside each other. Looking around the room for an empty seat, I found a vacant table at the front of the classroom and decided to sit there. Nicki caught the corner of my eye, as I walked to the table. She glared in my direction, then whispered to her fellow cheerleaders. Their laughter echoed across the room.

Mr. Martinez swung the door back and entered the classroom. "Welcome back, students," he began, setting his books on the podium, once he reached the front of the room. He turned his back to us, holding a green marker to the board as he began to write out his name. "If you have not had one of my classes before, my name is Mr. Martinez." I looked down at the thick textbook on the table in front of me, losing focus when he continued with the introduction.

"Is this room 302?" A voice interrupted Mr. Martinez in the middle of his speech. I lifted my head at the sound of it. I knew that voice.

"Tom! Yes, I'm sorry I left you waiting downstairs," Mr. Martinez said. "Class, we have a new student joining us this semester, Tom Sutton." Mr. Martinez gestured in the boy's direction. "I trust that you all will do your best to make Tom feel welcome. Why don't you take a seat up here in the front, by Addie?"

I froze, too afraid to look into his eyes and acknowledge the truth.

Tom sat down beside me, in the chair to my left. I turned my head, though only slightly. He smiled at me, and then nodded his head in politeness. I looked away, refocusing on Mr. Martinez's lesson for the day. When the sign-in sheet made its way to our table, I let him write his signature first. Tom pushed the piece of paper towards me. I grabbed it without meeting his eyes, making sure that our hands did not touch.

When class ended, I packed my bag, then waited in silence. Tom stared at me and refused to move, even though I wanted nothing more than for him to leave quietly. Unable to stand the tension any longer, I rose from the table and took one last glimpse of him before I left. His eyes were the color of honey.

* * *

British literature class felt much less restricting. Mrs. White softly trotted across the front of the room, passing out the reading list for the semester. We would be reading *The Strange Case of Dr. Jekyll and Mr. Hyde*, *The Picture of Dorian Gray*, *Dracula*, and *The Woman in White*. I smiled down at the book titles. I had already read them all.

Afterwards, I stopped by the bathroom to splash cool water on my face. Someone had turned the heat up in the building, and I had grown hot in my thick gray sweater. I grabbed a few paper towels from the dispenser to dry my hands, and then looked in the mirror as I tied my hair back into a ponytail.

"Addie could never be homecoming queen." I immediately knew that the voice belonged to Nicki. I rushed towards the nearest bathroom stall and closed the door.

"Why not?" It was the voice of a cheerleader, though I couldn't be sure which one. They all sounded the same to me.

"The same reason why Ricky would never go out with her," Nicki chimed. "She's not pretty."

I felt my brow furrow in response. A cold

feeling came over me, despite the sweat that had collected at the ridge of my palms. I listened for them to leave, and then bolted once they had. I didn't look in the mirror.

Chapter 3

Thankfully, Nicki was not in my next class, but Ricky was. I walked to the front of the classroom, standing in line behind the other students. Mr. Mason was a complete stickler about the seating chart. On the first day of class, he posted the chart at the front of the classroom, with the seats facing the opposite direction on the paper. So, everyone usually ended up seating themselves in the mirror image of the actual seating chart, because the angle he used to lay it out was just too confusing.

I followed a group of students to the back of the classroom, keeping my head down, as I looked at the seat number that was assigned to my name. I had written it down in my notebook, but all I noticed was the sketch of Tom's eyes that I had drawn earlier. I stopped in the fourth row, behind a very recognizable head of black hair.

"Ricky," I spoke with a sharp edge to my voice. "What are you doing in my seat?"

He turned around, but the "he" was not Ricky. The boy in my seat was Tom.

"Oh," I chirped, too startled to keep quiet. "I'm sorry. I thought you were—"

"Your seat is behind mine," he interrupted. Tom quickly glanced into my eyes, offering a hint of the yellow-gold in his.

I sank down into the chair, accepting the fact that I would have to stare at the back of his head for the next fifty minutes. Mr. Mason entered the room, clapping his hands together as he did so. He was not a very tall man, and his thin, wiry body most closely resembled a toothpick.

"Pop quiz!" Mr. Mason exclaimed, running to his desk. He picked up a thick stack of papers, while I sighed in misery. "Mr. Travis," he declared, "nice of you to join us."

I turned back in my seat, cringing when Ricky sat down in the desk behind me. He pressed his lips out, kissing the air in front of him. I handed him a quiz over my shoulder, once the remaining pages for our row reached me.

"Hey Mr. Mason!" Ricky leaned over my shoulder. "Can I borrow a pencil?"

"Sure," the teacher replied. Mr. Mason opened his desk drawer to retrieve a pencil. Without any foreseen warning, he threw the pencil at Ricky, and it hit him in the head.

"Ow!" Ricky scratched his head. "What was that for?"

"Maybe next time you should come to class

more prepared, Mr. Travis." Mr. Mason paced the floor, walking up and down every row. "I will not tolerate coming to class unprepared!" He stopped in front of Ricky's desk, hovering over him. "Even from the star quarterback," he added. Then, Mr. Mason lowered his voice, and only those around him heard what he had to say next. "Football season's over Ricky. Get a clue."

I chuckled to myself, making a mental note to remember the day Ricky Travis got showed up in trigonometry class. "What are you laughin' at?" Ricky tapped my shoulder with his pencil. I turned my head, offering a sassy smirk. "Mr. Mason, Addie's cheating off my quiz!" Ricky yelled in the tone of a tattle-telling preschooler.

"There's nothing written on your page yet, Mr. Travis," Mr. Mason said from the front of the room, though his back was turned to us. I laughed a little louder this time, holding a hand over my mouth to muffle the noise.

Just as I bent my head down to start the quiz, Ricky grabbed the ponytail at the back of my head and forcefully jerked it out of place. My neck slammed into the desk behind me as I cried out in pain. All of my hair fell down in thick, wavy locks, while Ricky continued tugging it at the ends.

Enraged, Tom rose from his desk and leapt on top of Ricky. By the time I was able to sit up in my own desk and look at what was happening, the two boys were on the floor, brawling. I held a hand to the back of my neck, overcome by a sudden migraine.

Ricky pinned Tom to the ground, battering his fist against Tom's face. Mr. Mason rushed to the back of the room, leaping over desks like an Olympic hurdler. But before Mr. Mason could reach them, Tom jabbed Ricky with a strong arm, and that was when Ricky's nose started bleeding.

Mr. Mason grabbed both of the boys by their shirt collars and marched them out the door, down the hall, and into the principal's office. When he returned, Mr. Mason collected the quizzes whether we had finished them or not. I hadn't answered a single question.

* * *

Before gym class started, I changed clothes in the locker room and tied my hair back into a ponytail. Afterwards, I followed a group of junior girls onto the track. I heard them complaining about the cold, but I liked the winter weather. It was nice to see my breath in the open air before me.

Coach Coleman appeared with a group of junior boys, both Ricky and Tom among them. Ricky had a light brown bandage covering his nose, while Tom wore a strip of white tape over his cheekbone. Suddenly, it felt as if everyone's eyes were on me.

"All right, kids," Coleman began. "Run five. Walk five." Coleman lifted a silver whistle to his lips, signaling the start of our laps. Ricky sat down on a row of bleachers, touching his nose in agony. "That's all right, son," Coleman said. "You can sit out the first week."

Coleman was the varsity football coach. Go figure.

My classmates rushed by in a blur of skin and clothing, as I caught a glimpse of Tom dressed in a black t-shirt and black sweatpants, with a white pin-stripe on either side of them. He walked past me, quietly staring into my eyes, before turning his head and running after the others. Bewildered, I shook my head and shrugged, because the boy from my dream was the same one who was distracting me now in gym class.

Coach Coleman noticed the distraction and came running after me, blowing his whistle all the while. I chased after Tom, hurriedly escaping the wrath of Coleman. When I caught up with Tom, he looked over his shoulder at me.

"Hi," I softly greeted. "I just wanted to thank you for what you did, earlier today." I motioned over my shoulder at the bleachers, where Ricky sat holding his nose.

"So now you'll talk to me." Tom kept a steady pace, breathing deeply. "That's right." Tom snapped his fingers and looked up at the sky. "You're one of those who has to be rescued first."

I exhaled, looking to the football field that rested in the middle of the track. "How did things go in the principal's office?"

Tom turned his head towards me. "Fine," he

said. "How does your neck feel?"

"Fine," I echoed. We both started laughing at that. After another half mile of keeping pace with him, I worked up the nerve to tell Tom that I had seen him before today.

"So, this is going to sound so crazy, but..." I hesitated, not wanting him to think that I needed to seek mental help. Tom looked back and forth, between me and the track, until I spoke again. "I had a dream about you. I was at this dance that our school has every year, in December, and-"

"I know," he interjected before I could go on.

"You know?" I stopped on the track, tugging at his shirt sleeve to make him stop with me. "How could you possibly know?"

Tom stood before me, leaning his face towards mine. I could feel his breath on my lips. "Because you weren't dreaming." Tom took off running again, as the rest of the gym class came barreling towards me. I stepped back at the sight of the stampede and fell into the end zone on the football field.

Before I could regain my bearings, Coach Coleman ran after me, whistle in hand. Frantic, I jumped to my feet and sprinted onto the track with a hand over each ear.

Chapter 4

After gym class, I changed back into my school clothes and headed to the cafeteria. I saw Tom up ahead, on the breezeway, walking with his hands stuffed into his pockets. He was alone.

Picking up the pace, I hurried after him, enjoying the sight of my breath misting in the air. I watched him enter the building and flinched when the door slammed shut behind him.

Just before I reached the entryway, Ricky appeared out of thin air. "Hey Addie," he beckoned, sliding his arm behind my neck. "Where ya goin'?"

"Stop touching me," I demanded, pulling myself out of his grasp. I entered the cafeteria and searched for Tom in the crowd. Grabbing a sand-colored lunch tray, I followed the handrails until I had reached the back of the line. I quickly spotted Tom and smiled. There were only two middle-school boys standing between us.

Once I reached the long, buffet-styled food

station, I grabbed a turkey sandwich, carrot sticks, a fruit cup, and a bowl of banana pudding, and then placed them each on the tray in that order. Moving along in the line, I waited to grab a bottle of water, until the two boys between Tom and me scampered off, in search of the soda fountain.

Tom spoke over the protective layer of glass that covered the food, asking the lunch lady for a fork. "They're over there," I butted in, pointing to the table by the soda fountain. It was covered with silverware and condiments. The lunch lady nodded, pointing in the same direction.

"Thank you," Tom said, looking at the lunch lady. He turned to me and nodded before walking off.

"Hey girl." Ricky stood behind me with a tray of hamburgers, potato chips, and Snickers bars. How he was able to maintain his clear complexion with that kind of diet was a mystery that I had never been able to solve.

I grabbed a small milk carton from the food line and peeled the opening back before setting the carton down on my lunch tray. Ricky placed his hands around my waist and squeezed my stomach with his muscular arms. "Ricky, let go," I whimpered, barely able to breathe. I could feel his hot breath against my neck. The stubble of his beard felt tingly and strange against my skin. "Leave me alone," I complained, while students stopped and stared.

Ricky picked up the bowl of banana pudding

from my tray and poured it all over my hair. I froze, pulling my fingers through the creamy yellow substance. The pudding dripped down my face, falling into my eyes and mouth. In anger, I picked up the milk carton and poured it down his shirt. Ricky's eyes widened as the stinging cold liquid ran down his chest.

I smirked in his direction, then puckered my lips into a fake kiss, mimicking his earlier behavior in Mr. Mason's class. Instantly provoked, Ricky grabbed the back of my ponytail and pulled, sending me to my knees. I slapped his arms and screamed to be let go, until I felt two arms wrap around my stomach and pull me away from him. But Ricky pursued me anyway, while I flailed around, eventually kicking him in the jaw. When I did, Ricky staggered backwards and sank down to the floor in front of me.

Tom still had his arms around me when Principal Caldwell approached us with a clipboard in hand. "You three," he coldly commanded, pointing to each of us. "Follow me."

Tom helped me to my feet and glared at Ricky before we all followed the principal back to his office. Ricky walked beside Caldwell, talking with him the whole time as if they were old pals. Principal Caldwell was Nicki's father; it was so unfair. But I forced myself to be quiet, and even bit my tongue, to keep from yelling the obscenities that I was thinking in my head.

When we reached Caldwell's office, he sat

down in a brown leather office chair that rolled in front of his desk, a nice piece of furniture with a cherry oak finish. "Which one of you would like to tell me what happened this time?" Caldwell looked me in the eye. "Addie?"

We stood before him in a row of three. Somehow, I had been sandwiched in between Tom and Ricky. The former stood to my right, the latter to my left.

I cleared my throat, reminding myself that Caldwell would favor Ricky above all else because of Nicki. "Well, we were in the lunch line and Ricky attacked me."

"What?" Ricky intercepted. "That's not true. She attacked me," Ricky pleaded, motioning to the bloody nose that Tom had given him in math class and the swollen jaw that I had given him ten minutes ago. I lunged for Ricky's throat, disgusted with him for lying, because I knew that he would get away with it. Caldwell would see to that.

Tom pulled me away from Ricky and into his grasp. With his arms locked around my clavicle, Tom held me back to prevent me from pouncing on Ricky again.

"Let her go," Caldwell demanded. Tom released me, and then stepped in front of Ricky, taking my place between them. Caldwell gripped a pen in his hand and pointed it at me. "Detention," he said, sending a soft heat through my body. Then, he raised the pen towards Tom and did the same. "Detention," he repeated.

"What about him?" Tom and I said in unison. Ricky held his nose, complaining that it had started bleeding again.

"Ricky," Caldwell addressed him, though without the condescending pen. "I want a five page paper on the importance of Southern hospitality, due on Friday."

"What?" I argued, leaning over Caldwell's desk. "We get detention and all he has to do is write a paper!" I motioned from us to Ricky as the sentence lengthened.

"Ms. Smith, let's see," Caldwell sputtered, opening a file on his desk. "You're eligible for that art program, at the institute in Atlanta this summer. Is that correct?"

"Yes sir," I answered, resenting the scruples that require one to respect authority.

"Wouldn't want to spoil your chances now, would you?" Caldwell raised a gray eyebrow, while his sinister gray eyes failed to blink.

"No sir," I spoke through my teeth, holding my hands behind my back to keep from strangling him.

"Well then." He smiled, revealing two crooked front teeth. "I suggest that you apologize to Mr. Travis, and then be on your merry way."

I turned to Ricky, sighing in discontent. Tom grabbed my wrist and then spoke into my ear. "Just do it," he whispered, nudging me on.

"I'm sorry, Ricky," I offered, then quickly averted my eyes.

"That's all right," Ricky remarked. "We all make mistakes. Isn't that right, Tom?"

Tom kept his hand around my wrist, sensing that my blood had yet to stop boiling.

"All right," Caldwell said. "Off you go." He pointed towards the door, prompting us to leave. "Oh, and take a shower." Caldwell waved a hand in front of his nose. "Ya'll smell like food."

Ricky left first, and then we sauntered out afterwards. Caldwell slammed the door behind us, just as I crossed the threshold. Tom walked with me down the hallway, shoving his hands into his pockets.

"I can't believe that guy," Tom snapped, kicking one of his black boots into the side of the wall. "Does Ricky always get out of trouble so easily?"

"Yes," I complained, running a hand through my hair. It felt sticky and gross.

"Man, my first day at a new school and I've already got detention," he said, studying the floor beneath him.

"How mad are your parents going to be when you get home?" I searched his face and smiled when he found mine.

"They shouldn't be too mad," he began. "They died when I was a little boy. I never knew my parents." Tom grew quiet, looking through the glass windows at the end of the hallway.

"Tom, I'm so sorry," I sympathized, holding my palm to my chest. "I didn't know." Tom nodded, as if the matter were of no importance. "What about your parents? Will they be mad?"

"Oh yeah," I chuckled, "Mom's gonna flip."

Chapter 5

Addison Elizabeth Smith!"

A cold shiver came over me at the sound of Mom's voice. "Yes Mother." I entered the foyer with a backpack slung over my shoulder. We never spoke this formally to each other, unless I had gotten into trouble. Mom was great about paying attention to me when things were going badly. She never said anything when they weren't.

"Please tell me why I received a call from the principal's office today," she snapped, still dressed in scrubs.

"Hey Mom." I waved. "It's good to see you too."

"Cut that out right now." She pointed her finger at me, reminiscent of Caldwell. "You served detention today?"

"Yeah, so?" I opened the pantry, searching for something crunchy to eat.

"You've never served detention in your entire life, Addie. This just doesn't sound like you at all," she murmured, placing her hands on her hips.

"It's Ricky, Mom," I insisted, turning from the pantry to face her.

"Who?" A fine line formed between her eyebrows. Two pairs of crow's feet crinkled at the outer edges of her eyelids.

"Ricky Travis," I hesitated, "the quarterback."

"Oh yeah." She moved towards the telephone as it began to ring. "He's cute." She grinned like a Cheshire cat. "Hello?" Mom and I don't really look anything alike. She has deep brown eyes, dark brunette hair, and olive skin, convincing me that I must have inherited my lighter features from someone else in the family. "Yes, I'll be right in," she declared and hung the phone back up on the wall.

"Back to the hospital?" I lifted myself onto the counter, letting my legs dangle beneath me.

"Yes." She looked down at the cell phone in her hand as she left the kitchen. "A cesarean and then two sets of twins," she announced. "I'm staying in town tonight. I only stopped by to stock the fridge with more food." We lived in the country, on a plot of sixty beautiful acres. Funny thing is, I was the only one who noticed.

"What about Dad?" I walked behind her, following her footsteps like a house dog.

"He's got that deposition in Atlanta tomorrow, and then court for the rest of the week." She did not look up from her phone when she reached the front door.

"Goodbye, Mom," I called after her. She crossed the threshold, already talking to someone else on the phone again. The door slammed shut behind her. "Love you," I whispered to myself. It wasn't like she was going to hear me.

Every night had been like this since I turned thirteen, when I was old enough to stay at home by myself. I looked in the fridge. Mom had stopped by an Italian restaurant, a Chinese restaurant, and a Mexican restaurant and ordered enough food for a week. Everything looked delicious, but I wasn't hungry.

I watched TV in the living room for a little while, flipping to a new channel each time a commercial came on. Any homework that had been assigned was due later in the week, since today was the first day back at school. So, I headed upstairs to my bedroom and picked up the phone.

I had been trying to get in touch with Eric all week, since he never showed up at the dance. We had been friends since childhood, but when his sister Emily went missing two years ago, the entire family moved to Atlanta. I understood the need for a change, because Emily had been my best friend.

"Eric," I sighed in relief, glad to hear the sound of his voice.

"Hi Addie," he replied, cheerful enough.

"What happened to you at the dance? You never showed up. I've been trying to get a hold of you all week." I sat in the chair by my window, rubbing a thumb over my fingernails.

"Sorry Addie, I got held up." Eric grew quiet, pensive even. Neither of us said anything on the phone for a long time, until he broke the silence. "Mom and Dad don't want me coming back to Savannah anymore," Eric murmured.

"What?" I could not believe it. Eric was the only piece of Emily that I had left.

"They don't think it's safe." I could hear him breathing in the background.

"Okay," I accepted. "I understand."

"Be careful, Addie," Eric said before hanging up the phone.

"I will."

* * *

Back at school, Mr. Mason rearranged the seating chart. Ricky and I were now separated by three rows of desks. It was nice to let my hair down.

Jeanine joined me for lunch on Friday, complaining about life as a freshman. I gave her advice, recalling my experience with the same teachers and courses. Jeanine was a sweet girl, with her cute childlike features. Except for the black hair, I did not see how she and Ricky were related.

"Have you seen my lipstick?" Jeanine opened her purse and began sifting through every pocket.

"No," I replied. Jeanine wore a cherry red shade of color on her lips. It was as much a part of her look as the black bob.

"It's okay." She waved her hand in the air, tossing the matter aside. "I have another one at home."

At the end of the day, Jeanine approached me on the way to our lockers. "What are you doing this weekend?" Her dark blue eyes glistened beneath the fluorescent lighting.

"I don't have any plans. What did you have in mind?" I held a notebook and two textbooks in my arms, as we neared my locker.

"I was thinking we could go see a movie," Jeanine offered, a desperate look in her eyes.

"Yeah," I agreed. "That sounds fun."

We paused in the hallway and noticed a group of teenage boys hovering around my locker. I recognized them as members of the varsity football team and close friends of Ricky. "Excuse me," I demanded, forcing my way through the crowd.

The group of boys parted like the Red Sea, splitting into two clusters, as I saw what lay between them. On the front of my gray metal locker, the word **VIRGIN** was written in red lipstick. I recognized the shade as the one Jeanine wore on her lips: cherry red.

I turned around and gave Jeanine a questioning look. "I didn't do it," she said, shaking her head from side to side. The ends of her black bob swayed to and fro.

Nicki stepped out from the girls' bathroom with her hands crossed over her chest. Her platinum blonde ringlets jostled with each forceful step of her high-heeled boots. I could make out the image of a small object in her hand that was the size of a chess piece. Nicki approached Jeanine and dropped the object before her feet. It was a tube of cherry red lipstick.

Tom appeared out of the corner of my eye. He took a slow step forward, looking at my locker and then turning his face to look at me. Jeanine knelt down, retrieving the tube of the lipstick from the floor.

"Thanks," Nicki sneered. She smiled down at Jeanine before turning to walk away.

I scowled in Jeanine's direction and stormed off, not bothering to stop by my locker. "Addie," Tom crooned. He grabbed my arm when I passed him, but I pulled away and bolted for the door.

"I didn't do it Addie!" Jeanine yelled after me, but I wasn't in the mood to listen. "Addie! I didn't do it!"

I spent the afternoon holed up in my bedroom, distracting myself with chemistry homework. I neither liked it nor understood it, but it took my mind off what had happened that day.

Before sunset, I trudged down our long dirt driveway. The mailbox stood at the end of it, on the other side of our locked gate. I hopped over the shortest part of the gate and checked the mail. I was the only one who ever did.

I found a handful of bills, two fliers advertising

the opening of a new pizza place in town, and one envelope addressed to me. I hopped back over the gate and folded the rest of the mail into a wad that was small enough to fit inside my jacket pocket.

A cool chill filled the air as I veered off the driveway, entering the wilderness. I walked with the envelope in my hand, striving to get as deep into the forest as possible. Once I felt secure enough, within the safety of the woods, I sat down at the base of a massive oak tree and opened the envelope. There was a folded piece of printer paper inside.

Confusion swept over me, because there was no return address on the back of the envelope. I scanned the stretch of wilderness surrounding me to make sure that no one else could see what I held in my hands.

I unfolded the sheet of paper and held a hand over my mouth. A pair of emerald green eyes stared back at me. I was looking at the portrait from my dream. Three words were scrawled in black ink at the bottom of the page: *Find the necklace.*

I folded the portrait into a small square and slid it into my pocket with the rest of the mail. Rising to my feet, I brushed away any dirt that had collected on the back of my clothing and headed for the house. I stopped along the way, watching the sun sink into the trees. Before the sunset was complete, a melodic harmony filtered through the woods. My ears perked up at the sound, so I followed it.

I soon found myself trailing beside the wooden fence that separated our land from the neighboring property. A row of trees lined the fence on the other side, so I wasn't able to see what lay beyond the border until I reached an open gap that spread into a stretch of pasture land. A man stood in the grass, no more than a hundred yards from me. He stared at the horizon, whistling to himself in glee.

"Tom?" I shouted in disbelief.

He turned around and lifted his hand in the air. "Hey," Tom called, walking towards the fence.

"What are you doing?" I leaned over the wooden railing, surprised by his presence.

"Just watchin' the sunset," he answered. Tom shoved his hands into his pockets and smiled in my direction.

"No," I clarified, "I mean, what are you doing here?"

Tom removed one hand from his pocket and slung it over the fence. "I live here," he said, as if it had always been true.

"Oh," I retorted. "Since when?" I had never known of anyone owning the lot next to us; it had always been vacant.

"My grandfather has a house here and I live with him." Tom's eyes glowed like the flames of a fire. The yellow edges of his irises appeared gold in the fading sunlight.

"Oh." I nodded. I remembered the envelope

in my pocket, and it suddenly felt bigger. "While I have you here, I need to show you something." I reached into my jacket pocket and unfolded the picture. Tom held his hand over the fence and took the page when I offered it to him. "Now," I murmured, lowering my voice. "I think it's about time we talked about that dream."

Chapter 6

Tom and I approached his grandfather's three-story colonial style mansion. Ivory pillars stood in a perfect row at the front of the porch, which wrapped all the way around the house. The front door was painted in coal black, to match the trim and shutters that framed each window.

"Are you coming?" Tom beckoned from the doorway.

"Oh," I started, climbing the few steps up to the entrance. Tom shut the door behind me and walked down the hallway that extended from the foyer. I glanced into the entryway of the dining room and sitting area as we passed through the house. Fine furniture and décor had been artistically laid out in each room, while numerous landscapes lined the walls on either side of us. I had never seen so many paintings in someone's house in all my life.

Tom turned right at the end of the hall. I

looked back over my shoulder to observe the kitchen as we passed it. Tom weaved his way through the dining room before entering the staircase that rested on the other side of the doorway. I followed Tom, taking two steps at a time to match his pace.

At the top of the staircase, I noticed a bedroom that sat snuggly in the right hand corner. But Tom turned in the other direction and stopped before an old wooden door. Tom jerked at the metal handle, sighing in relief when the door squeaked open.

We entered the dark room. It had no more light than what filtered through the small square window. A wooden board creaked beneath my feet when I took a step forward. "Can I see the picture?" Tom stuck his hand out. I unfolded the paper and handed it to him.

The original hung on the wall that lay just past the window. Tom held up the page beside the portrait. The two images were nearly identical in every way, except for the handwritten message at the bottom of the photocopy I had received in the mail.

"Who is she?" I stepped in front of the painting and rubbed my finger over the canvas, to feel the texture of the paint. A thin silver chain hung around the woman's neck, holding the stone over her breast. White diamonds circled the shape of the emerald, as it lay over her white satin gown.

"Antoinette Beaumont," Tom answered. He

pointed at the base of the painting, where a tiny string of letters spelled her name.

"So, whoever sent this wants me to find her necklace?" I nodded to the portrait. Tom handed the printed picture back to me and shoved his hands into his pockets.

"That's what it sounds like," Tom sighed, glancing over the painting one last time.

"Well, why did they send it to me? And how am I supposed to figure out who this person even is?" I folded the picture and put it back in my pocket. The door creaked open, startling me as I moved closer to Tom.

"I know who sent you that picture." A stranger stood in the doorway.

"Grandpa," Tom called, walking towards him. "I thought you were lying down." Tom placed his hand on the old man's chest. His face looked worn and ragged, with saggy, wrinkled skin bordering his eyes and mouth. But there was a look of intrigue in his beady blue eyes that could not be missed.

"Let me see her," the old man hissed. Tom stepped out of the way and motioned for me to come closer.

I swallowed, and then took three careful steps toward him. The old man placed his hand on my cheek and studied my eyes. I froze, widening my eyes at Tom when his grandfather began to examine a lock of my hair.

"All right, Grandpa." Tom grabbed his

grandfather by the shoulders and turned him towards the window. The old man sat down on the windowsill and patted his head with a white handkerchief.

"Mr. Sutton?" I asked, growing bold enough to step into the moonlight.

"Please, call me Daniel," he insisted.

"Okay, Daniel," I paused, holding my hands together in a nervous manner. Tom nodded in my direction, urging me to continue. "Who sent me this picture?" I handed him the piece of paper, which was now covered with wrinkles and creases.

Daniel removed a pair of reading glasses from his breast pocket and slipped them on. After quickly scanning the picture, he returned it to me and said, "Tony DeMilo."

"Tony DeMilo," I repeated, letting the words roll off my own tongue to see if they sounded any more familiar. I shook my head, knowing that they didn't. "Who's Tony DeMilo?"

"He was Antoinette's husband," Tom said. "She was murdered fifty years ago, right here in Savannah. They found her body floating in the river."

"Who killed her?" My heart was pounding. It sounded like it had settled at the base of my throat.

"Well, no one really knows for sure." Tom embellished the length of his words. I didn't like the tone of his voice; it was uncertain.

"I know." Daniel looked out the window, as if

the glass were allowing him to see into the past.

"DeMilo," I guessed, turning my head from Tom to his grandfather. "Am I right?"

"Yes," Daniel whispered, disliking the truth.

"How did you know them?" I could not fight the urge to learn more. I had to know what happened in Savannah all those years ago.

"Antoinette was friends with my wife." Daniel looked down at his wrinkled hands, as they began to shake. "I think I better go lie down," he said reluctantly. "I've excited myself too much this evening."

Tom helped Daniel to his feet and said, "You need to take it easy, Grandpa." Daniel shook his head, not wanting to hear it. "Wait here," Tom said to me, "and I'll walk you home." I nodded, watching as Tom led his grandfather through the doorway.

I circled the room until Tom returned. There was a door at the back of the room, concealed beneath a layer of darkness. I had never noticed it before.

"Let's go," Tom called. I turned my face away from that far secluded space in the room and followed Tom's voice into the hall. He didn't say anything about Daniel, so I didn't either.

Tom grabbed a thick winter coat from a wooden rack in the foyer and slipped his arms through the sleeves. I stuck my hands into the gray jacket over my sweater, preparing for the cold. As we entered the wilderness, our boots crunching over dried leaves and branches, I looked to Tom and asked, "Do you know why DeMilo killed his wife?"

"No," he replied, looking straight ahead.

"Liar," I murmured. Tom stopped, jerking his face in my direction.

"Antoinette is the lady in the painting," Tom snapped, his words rushing past my face in foggy, white breaths. "She was married to DeMilo, and he murdered her. That's all I know." Tom turned his back to me and continued through the woods. I remained where I stood.

"I don't believe you," I softly spoke.

Tom stopped dead in his tracks. "Look, it's not my story to tell, all right?" He turned back to me, his face dim and gray in the moonlight. "Come back another time." I accepted, nodding my head in the darkness.

We continued through the trees without speaking. I found the silence to be louder than the shrieking owl in the distance. Once we reached the edge of my house, I looked up at Tom. "You sure know your way around these parts," I mentioned. Tom ignored what I said and stopped before the front door steps. When he turned to walk away, I asked, "Can we talk?"

Tom hesitated, rocking back on his heels. I detected the faintest glimmer of gold in his eyes as he searched my face, considering. "I really should be getting back to Grandpa," he explained.

"It will only take a minute," I urged, motioning

for him to come to the door when I opened it. Tom tilted his head back, taking in the exterior of the house.

When he finally answered, it was through a pair of chattering teeth. "Oh, all right," he consented.

I shut the door behind us, placed the mail from my pocket on the kitchen table, and then walked into the living room. "My room's this way," I said, pointing towards the staircase in the distance.

"Where are your parents?" I sensed the uneasiness in Tom's voice. We climbed up the stairs, while I explained their absence.

"Working," I chirped. "Mom's a doctor. Dad's a lawyer." I rattled my parent's occupations off like a drive-thru attendant at a fast food restaurant: *Two cokes, two fries. Will that complete your order?*

I opened my bedroom door, flipped the light switch on, and sat down on the edge of my bed to remove the warm winter boots I had been wearing. "They have an apartment in town," I continued, tugging at the laces. "They bought it a few years ago, so they wouldn't have to drive out here late at night, if either of them had to stay late at work." Tom stalled in the doorway, unsure if he was allowed to enter. "They stay there most nights, so I don't wait up."

Tom stepped into the room, content that no disgruntled parent would come barging in at any moment. "That seems unfair," Tom mused, studying the drawings on my desk and the cork board above it. I left my boots on the floor in front of my bed and rose to shut the door.

"What does?" I unzipped my jacket and hung it up in the closet. Then, I grabbed my boots from the floor and threw them in the closet before shutting it.

Tom shed his thick winter coat and sat down in the chair by the window. "They ignore you," he declared, as if there were no question. I grew quiet, sitting down in the swivel chair before my desk. "I didn't mean it like that," Tom said, backpedaling. "What did you want to talk about?" Tom leaned forward in the chair, resting his elbows against his knees.

"What happened on the night of the dance?" I crossed one leg over the other, determined to have an answer. When he wouldn't respond, I pressed him further. "I know you were there."

"I wasn't," he argued, folding his arms over his chest. When I groaned in frustration, Tom spoke again. "You really don't remember, do you?" he asked, searching my face.

"All I can remember is being at the dance, and then I was in the room we just left at your grandfather's house. And you were there with the painting. Then I woke up here," I declared, looking at my bed against the wall. "That's all I can remember," I admitted, holding a palm to my forehead. When I tried to recollect anymore about that night, my temples began to throb.

Tom stared at me, his eyes like two glowing beams of light.

"Well," I grumbled, "are you going to tell me what happened or not?"

"Not tonight," he muttered. Tom sat still beneath the moonlight. I glared at him and let my shoulders sag in disappointment. But then a bolt of energy surged through my veins. I had an idea.

"Can I draw you?" I almost laughed at the idea myself. In that moment, nothing seemed more out of place.

"Um." Tom pulled his eyebrows together, thinking to himself. "Sure."

I opened my sketch pad to a fresh sheet of paper. There was a wooden box of colored pencils stored in the top drawer of my desk. I selected shades of black, yellow, gold, and brown from the box and set those pencils by the sketch pad on my desk.

"Just sit still," I told him. "And try not to breathe." Tom widened his eyes in alarm. I laughed, and then explained that I was only joking.

Chapter 7

A loud clatter woke me the next morning. I recognized that the sound was coming from the kitchen and leapt from the bed. My parents were home.

I opened my bedroom door and took the stairs down two at a time, not bothering to change out of the clothes I had slept in. I entered the kitchen, noticing the blender on the counter. It was filled with carrots, tomato juice, blueberries, and ice.

"Hey Dad," I spoke, recognizing his figure on the ground, kneeling behind an open cabinet door. Dad hit his head on the wood and peered around the door.

"You scared me," he barked, pressing a palm to the top of his head. "Have you seen the lid to this thing?" Dad shut the cabinet door and stood up, blood rushing to his face. I opened one of the overhead cabinets next to the fridge and grabbed the lid to the blender. "Thanks," Dad said. He took the lid from my hand and placed it over the blender.

I lifted myself onto the kitchen counter and watched the tornado of red, blue, and orange swirl inside the container. When the mixture became one frothy liquid concoction, Dad pressed a button that silenced the machine. "How is school?" Dad poured the drink into a thermos, then took a sip once it was full.

"Fine," I droned. Dad set the thermos down and cupped a hand over his mouth. The blended drink spewed from his lips, spraying across the floor. "Dad, what are you doing?" I slid down from the counter and retrieved a dish towel to wipe up the mess.

"That stuff's disgusting," he griped, rinsing his mouth out in the sink. "Your mother's insane," he said with his head bent under the faucet. I rolled my eyes, waiting for him to get out of the way, so I could clean the tile.

As if reading my mind, Dad stepped around the explosion of smoothie that remained on the floor, leaving it to me. There was a briefcase on the table, along with a jacket that completed his suit-and-tie ensemble. Dad was lucky to walk away with his work clothes unstained.

"How are you with money?" Dad slipped his arms through the jacket and straightened his tie. I stood with the dish towel in my hands, unsure of what he meant. "Oh, that reminds me," he began, reaching into his back pocket. "I just upgraded the credit card, and I don't think I gave you one yet."

An ash-blonde hair fell across his forehead, but he smoothed it back into place. "Just cut up the old one," he instructed, handing me a new piece of plastic from his wallet.

"Thanks," I muttered, carelessly tossing the credit card on the counter. Dad walked towards the front door, briefcase in hand, so I spoke up before he was gone. "Where's Mom?" I followed him into the foyer and leaned against the doorway.

"The hospital," he answered. "And then she leaves for that medical convention in the morning." He checked his appearance in the mirror hanging next to the coat rack. "Well," he chirped, "call us if you need anything." The door shut behind him in one swift, final movement.

I cleaned the kitchen floor and then did a load of laundry. There was an expired carton of milk in the fridge, so I poured it down the drain and wrinkled my nose at the smell. I wasn't living with parents. I was living with a couple of self-absorbed workaholics, who had forgotten that they had a kid of their own.

* * *

Sheets of sketching paper lay scattered across the desk in my bedroom. I pulled the center sheet towards me. It was the drawing of Tom that I had done the night before. It was mostly black-and-white, with empty spaces left for me to color in the rest of his skin, clothing, and eyes. I turned around in my swivel chair and looked at the window where Tom had been.

In the drawing, Tom sat with his arms relaxed and feet spread apart. He was wearing a charcoal sweater, with sleeves that stopped at the elbow, as well as a pair of black jeans and boots. The sweater dipped down into a v-shaped opening at the top of his chest. It revealed the olive tone of his skin, still glowing with traces of the summer sun, despite the change in season.

I picked up a flesh-colored pencil and sketched within the outline of his lips. I had made sure to copy them exactly as they were in real life. Tom was not smiling.

Looking at his eyes, I traced a rim around the deep black dots of each pupil. Then, I filled in the irises with a rich golden color and bubbled over them in yellow. I lowered my head over the paper and blew away any traces of pigment that the colored pencils had left behind.

I collected the other sheets of paper on my desk and stacked them into a pile. A small white envelope fell through the pages. It felt lighter than it had the day before, so I opened the flap of the envelope and looked inside. It was empty.

* * *

"Tom!" I stood on his front porch and beat my fist against the door. "Open up," I demanded, "it's Addie." A cream-colored shade flicked against one of the windows. "Come on!" I yelled. "I'm freezing out here!" The door opened.

"What?" Tom leaned against the door with a hand on his hip.

"Did you steal the picture DeMilo sent me?" I accused, raising my voice.

"Shh," he whispered, holding a finger to his lips. Tom grabbed my arm and jerked me across the threshold. "Be quiet," he said. Tom closed the door behind us and led me into the den. Beyond the arrangement of fine furniture, a well-lit fireplace sat snuggly against the far wall.

"Well," I continued, "did you steal it or not?" Tom parted his lips to reply, but then hesitated. "Just tell me," I demanded. "Did you take it?" Tom nodded. I turned away from him and headed towards the hallway. I was prepared to search every room in the house until I found it.

"Addie, wait," Tom called, "you don't understand." He caught the sleeve of my jacket and pulled me back. "I only did it to protect you." I searched his eyes, unsure if I could find truth in them.

"Protect me from what?" I snapped, drawing my arm out of his grasp. I marched into the hallway when he didn't respond.

"Look, it's complicated, all right?" Tom stood at the end of the hall. "It would be really hard for me to explain it to you," he sighed. I looked back at him and then attempted to ward off the sudden pain in my chest.

"Oh," I piped up, "so what you're saying is that I'm too stupid to understand." The words left me trembling. I could not stand still any longer.

"No," Tom dissented, "that's not what I'm saying at all." I weaved my way through the house and did not stop until I had found the staircase. "You won't find it up there." My hand froze where I had placed it on the railing. Tom leaned against the wall with his hands in his pockets.

"Then where is it?" I demanded, stepping down from the handful of stairs that I had managed to climb. Tom studied the ground as if a map of Southeast Asia had been sketched onto the floor, and he was looking for a port.

"I threw it in the fire," Tom murmured, no louder than a whisper. He didn't look me in the eye until the words were out of his mouth. I retraced my steps to the den and knelt down in front of the fireplace. Pieces of ash danced beneath the flames.

"You never should have opened that envelope." Tom placed his hand on the mantle and glanced down at the fire.

"And why not?" I rose from my crouched position on the carpet. I could feel Tom's eyes watching me, but I could not bear to look at him.

Tom shook his head and shoved both hands into his pockets. It was the exact way that Tom behaved every time he felt cornered. I trudged to the door in disappointment. "Addie, wait a minute. Where are you going?" I walked out into the night and wrapped my arms around my chest to hold in the heat from my clothing. It was a long walk through the wilderness, but I was happy to be free of him.

When I reached my house, Jeanine had already called five times. I clicked through the voicemail messages she had left me, before deleting them altogether. I didn't want to talk about it.

I climbed up the stairs and walked into my bedroom, shutting the door behind me. Then, I removed my coat and draped it over the back of my desk chair. The drawing of Tom lay beside a box of colored pencils on my desk. I picked up my sketchpad and placed it over the drawing, covering Tom's face.

A thumping sound startled me as I turned to find Tom perched in the tree outside my window. I took a deep breath to calm myself before I opened the window. "What are you doing?" I leaned against the window frame, appalled by his very presence.

"I wasn't done talking to you," Tom gasped, positioning himself over the highest branch of the tree. I could see his breath in white smoky puffs.

"You could have just called me," I suggested, "or knocked on the front door." I raised a thumb over my shoulder to indicate the entrance of the house.

"No," Tom replied. "Your mom's here." He sat down on the tree limb and let his legs dangle beneath him.

"What?" I raised my eyebrows in concern.

"No she's not," I insisted. "Mom's never home."

"Addie," Mom called. There was a knock on my bedroom door. "Addie," she repeated. "Who are you talking to in there?"

Tom smirked, as if to say, *See, I told you so.*

I scrambled, closing the window in a panic. Mom opened the door just as I turned around to face her. "Mom," I began, masking the surprise in my voice. "What are you doing home?"

"My flight got delayed and your dad left his laptop," she exhaled. Mom looked around my room and then walked towards me. I was still standing by the window.

"Oh," I said, "are you staying here tonight?" I knew that she wasn't listening to me, because her eyes studied the window pane like she had never seen glass before.

"No, I'm headed back to the airport in a bit." The words came out in a rush, so she could ask, "Who's that?" I swallowed, afraid that Tom had not concealed himself.

"Where?" I stepped back and made room for her as she approached the window. Mom gazed at the pane for a long moment, searching the tree.

"I thought I saw someone," she finally said, straightening her blouse into position over a pair of dress pants. "I guess not," she muttered unconvincingly.

"Dad's laptop is on the table in the living room." I followed her to the door, trying my best to get her out of my room. "I saw it after he left this morning," I added, wondering how cold Tom was on the branch outside my window.

"That's a good daughter," Mom mused. She patted me on the shoulder and then left me standing at the top of the staircase. I watched her from above as she slipped into her winter coat and collected the laptop. "Hey Addie!" she called. "Have you seen my red scarf?"

"It's on the coat rack, by the door," I answered. Mom walked in that direction and wrapped the scarf around her neck. And then, just like Dad, she was gone.

www.ingramcontent.com/pod-product-compliance
Lightning Source LLC
Chambersburg PA
CBHW020909200626
46814CB00001BA/245